Riding Scared

Marion Crook

D1453708

James Lorimer & Company, Publishers
Toronto, 1996

James Lorimer & Company Ltd. acknowledges with thanks the support of the Canada Council and the Ontario Arts Council in the development of writing and publishing in Canada.

The author wishes to thank the staff of the Maple Ridge Equestrian Centre for their help and advice.

Cover illustration: Ian Watts

Canadian Cataloguing in Publication Data

Crook, Marion, 1941–
Riding scared

(Sports stories)
ISBN 1-55028-531-9 (bound)
ISBN 1-55028-530-0 (pbk.)

I. Title. II. Series: Sports stories (Toronto, Ont.)

PS8555.R6116R5 1996   jC813'.54   C96-931677-1
PZ7.C76Ri 1996

James Lorimer & Company Ltd., Publishers
35 Britain Street
Toronto, Ontario
M5A 1R7
Printed and bound in Canada

Contents

To Rita Murray,
my technical advisor who loves horses

1

Runaway

Gillian stood perfectly still. She could hear the yells coming from the riding arena, the crack of wood breaking, the pounding of hooves on the sawdust.

"He's getting away! Stop him!" The shouts reached her and held her frozen in place, while she imagined a thousand pounds of mean horseflesh thundering down the alleyway toward her. The horse would trample her into the sawdust like a smashed bag of potato chips. She'd be in pieces on the ground, the pellets from her bucket scattered around her, while the horse careened on into the meadow and freedom.

She blinked when she saw her fantasy was a reality — big, black and heading straight for her.

"Gillian. Grab him!"

She really was going to be trampled! Gillian dropped her pail and stumbled backwards into the feed area, grasped the rungs nailed to the wall and climbed. She'd reached the hayloft when the horse raced by. Safe. She heard the pounding of hooves, then the crack and splinter of wood as the horse crashed through the gate.

"Gillian! Why didn't you stop him? Now I'll have to spend an hour chasing him in the meadow!" Mike Yardy stood at the bottom of the ladder, glaring up at her.

"I'm not getting in the way of half a ton of determination." Gillian descended hand-over-hand and dropped to the ground. "What happened? What made him spook?"

Mike ignored the question. "You're afraid of horses!" He stated the fact, sounding disgusted. "You shouldn't be here."

Anyone would have been afraid of that horse, Gillian thought. No one with any sense would get between it and freedom, but she had to agree with Mike; she was afraid of horses and she shouldn't be at the stable. Riding was her father's idea, not hers. Gillian wanted art and composition. Her father didn't agree. He thought she needed activity and competition — not that her father knew her very well. A new wife, new family and new town didn't make friendship with his thirteen-year-old daughter much of an option, but he was responsible and determined, and Gillian was enrolled in riding.

When she had agreed to the lessons, Gillian created beautiful pictures in her mind of peaceful ponies walking slowly through green meadows, the blue Coast Mountains of British Columbia in the background, miles of neat blueberry farms on one side, acres of tall forests on the other — and hours spent away from her mother and brother. Having to submit to riding lessons, riding clothes and constant reminders of how much money it all cost seemed a good trade-off. Gillian hadn't counted on being afraid. She hadn't known she was afraid until she was surrounded by big, menacing and unpredictable horses.

Horses were bad, but riders were worse. All the girls at the Maple Ridge stable had started riding lessons when they were nine years old. A thirteen year old was an old lady. They ignored her. Maybe they had all the friends they needed. Maybe she was too much of a beginner to be interesting to them. Maybe she should try harder. Maybe she should give up. After five months she had one good friend, Carley Mackenzie. The two of them had talked about horses, lessons, teachers, boys, parents and the psychic auras that interested Carley. Carley was a good rider and she thought Gillian was *going* to be a good rider, given time and practice.

"You're a natural," she had said. "You'll put Hawkeye over those jumps with no problem. All you need is practice and confidence."

All I need, Gillian thought, is to be sure that a horse isn't going to buck me off or knock me down.

Mike ran after his horse. Gillian picked up the pail and refilled it with pellets for Hawkeye, her horse, the one horse she liked. Hawkeye was a calm, reliable, *old* horse, almost as old as Gillian. He had been competing in jumping events since he was five years old and knew all the things about riding that Gillian didn't. Her dad had bought him on the advice of the stable instructor because he was a good "beginner's" horse. She didn't mind Hawkeye. When he was not in the riding ring, he moved slowly and almost seemed to listen when Gillian talked to him. She carried the pellets into the stable and poured them into his feed box.

"Hey, Gillian. Move it," Carley called into Hawkeye's stall. "The whole world of high-powered, complex, coordinated team strategy awaits us."

"What?" Gillian asked.

"We've got a meeting in five," Carley said more clearly.

"Where?" Gillian never seemed to hear about the riding instructor's impending meetings.

"In Julie's office. Come on. You can groom Hawkeye later."

Gillian hung the bucket on a nail. "Carley, why did Mike's horse spook that way?"

"Oh, you know Mike. He probably left the reins down and went off to take a picture with that new camera of his," Carley said. "Fury just took advantage of his freedom."

Gillian nodded. "Mike does forget details, doesn't he? Like closing a door, or tying up his horse."

"He probably thinks someone else should do it," Carley said.

Gillian petted Hawkeye's brown rump. He turned his big, dark eyes on her, then nosed back into the pellets. Food first. Affection later.

"Come on." Carley started down the alleyway between the stalls.

Gillian grabbed her notebook and rushed after her friend.

They entered the trainer's office together, Gillian trying to pretend that no one was staring at her. She flicked her long braid off her shoulder and looked for a place to sit. Carley stood beside her, as tall as she, her fair hair hanging straight, her blue eyes darting around the room looking for a comfortable spot. "Over there." She nodded to a couch in the corner.

Gillian was halfway across the room before she realized Mike occupied part of the couch. She took a deep breath and was proud of herself for not hesitating in her walk. She sat down. Carley grabbed the chair beside her. Mike turned his head slowly. "You should have caught Fury, wimp," he said softly. "You know *nothing* about horses and you're not learning fast enough." He looked down on her, fourteen years old and taller than any of the girls, sharp eyes, sharp features, sharp tongue. He faced Gillian with his back to the room so Julie couldn't hear him.

Gillian sat perfectly still, then blinked and stared at Mike. In her mind, she drew fine, baby curls around Mike's face. She added fullness to his cheeks, squashed his nose and took out two front teeth. Mike at six. A silly, bumbling, awkward boy. She would *not* let him bother her. She took another deep breath, let it out slowly and looked away.

"Great," Julie said, beaming at the assembled riders. Julie looked like an athlete; slender but with firm arm and leg muscles, short blond hair and bright blue eyes. She walked and stood as if she had energy she could barely contain, as if she would run or jump at any moment. Sometimes just being around her made Gillian feel tired.

"Everyone's here." Julie picked up a clipboard and read down a list attached to it. "Tomorrow's jumping event will be in Cloverdale. That's only a short drive, but the horses have to be just as carefully prepared as if they were going on a two-day haul: shipping bandages on their legs, fly sheets on their backs, clean trailers, the lot. This will be one of the three preliminary shows you need before the big show in Calgary. Remember, even if it seems to be a small competition, every show is important. Okay?"

Everyone nodded. They'd heard it before.

"I'm going to read out the classes and who is entered in what, so get your notebooks out and write down your times and class numbers. Gillian, this will be your first time. We're all rooting for you." She smiled at Gillian, who dutifully smiled back. It amazed Gillian that Julie could be so blind to the way the other girls felt about her. There was no one in this room rooting for her but Carley and Julie. Maybe Julie only understood horses who, Carley said, generally were neither cold nor complicated, at least not the way people were.

Gillian sighed and wished for the old days of last summer when she was free to paint, draw and listen to music, when the only energetic thing she did was swim in the pool with her friends. She had spent her usual two weeks at Dad's home and had brought her paints with her. Big mistake. Her dad thought painting was useless. She'd heard him on the phone to her mother.

"It's a competitive world out there. You're trying to bring up a sweet and spineless waif! She's got to toughen up, to fight for what she wants, to get out there and grab opportunities."

Gillian thought she had grabbed opportunities. She had put her name down for the extra art classes at school. She'd managed a summer session at the community program. She had the beginnings of a portfolio — she'd need to have an impressive one if she wanted to be accepted into the Art Academy after high school. But that didn't count as competition or ambition to her dad. Painting was a "hobby."

"Nice pictures," he'd said. Nice, but not important. "Riding," he'd told her mother. "That'll put some starch into her."

None of her friends rode horses. None of them could afford it. Riding was expensive, very expensive. Gillian wondered if the money her dad spent on riding lessons and the horse was his way of showing he was a "good dad." In lots of ways, he *was* a good dad.

"You might as well grab the chance," her mom had said. "I know I can't afford it on a teacher's salary. It's going to be difficult for me too because I'll have to keep Richard at school now."

Gillian had babysat her eight-year-old brother after school for a couple of years. Now she had to practise riding every day.

"If you have any questions," Julie was saying, "I'll answer them."

Mike wanted to know who would be renting part of his horse trailer. Julie consulted her list and told him, "Amanda will be travelling with you, so talk to her about it."

Mike nodded.

Then Julie said, "Gillian Cobb?"

Gillian paid attention.

"You'll be going with Carley, Gillian. Her mother asked that you do that regularly because she wants to haul the same horse every time. Is that okay?"

Gillian nodded with relief. Elizabeth Mackenzie, Carley's mom, was great. Carley was friendly, and she'd be safe from Mike — at least while she was travelling to and from the show. Anything could happen at the show.

2

Playday

Gillian met Carley and her mother Elizabeth at the stables at seven on Sunday morning. The recent rains had washed the dust from the shrubs and left raindrops glinting on the grass. The mountains seemed a deeper, more intense blue in the clear air, even a cobalt blue, Gillian thought.

"What I do for you two!" Elizabeth said as she climbed down from her truck. "I worked until three in the morning and here I am — conscious, competent and ready to chauffeur. I must be crazy."

"You probably are," Carley said. "Why did you work so late?"

"The painting was going so well." Elizabeth was an illustrator and worked in her home studio. She was the artist of Gillian's dreams: always painting and enthusiastic about it. She wore bright colours and fascinating jewellery. Today she wore jeans, a turquoise sweat shirt and no make-up. Dangling turquoise and silver earrings glinted in the morning sun. Sleepy brown eyes looked tolerantly at Gillian.

"Hi," Gillian said.

"Hi. Let's move these beasts. And please, don't be too cheerful. It's an indecent hour." Elizabeth shoved her wavy grey hair out of her eyes and walked with the girls toward the rear door of the trailer.

"Not enough caffeine in the veins," Carley confided to Gillian in an audible, theatrical whisper.

"Is she safe to drive?" Gillian answered in kind, glancing at Elizabeth.

The tiny lines at the edges of Elizabeth's eyes crinkled, and she smiled. "Just get those four-footed, pampered ponies out here and loaded — and don't criticize the hired help."

"Yes, ma'am. Immediately, ma'am." Carley spun around quickly, then ran with Gillian toward the stalls.

Hawkeye loaded easily. He had walked up ramps into trailers for years. Jupiter, Carley's horse, was not so placid. He shook his head and pranced a little at the bottom of the ramp. Gillian stayed well away from his feet. Hawkeye turned his head, looked back and snorted once. As if he had been commanded by the old horse, Jupiter stepped on the ramp and walked in.

The Cloverdale Arena was only thirty miles from Maple Ridge, one point of a triangle that included Maple Ridge and the big city of Vancouver. The rural communities around Vancouver supported many equestrian shows. That meant riders could take part without having to travel tiring distances.

Elizabeth drove slowly through the country back roads, so it was forty-five minutes before they arrived.

When Gillian first saw the exhibition grounds through the truck window, the horses looked to her like a set of toy farm animals that someone had carelessly thrown on the ground. Horses were everywhere in the parking lot and on the grass nearby. When Gillian climbed down from the truck, the horses seemed to enlarge and come alive. Some backed out of trailers; some shifted restlessly in place while owners unwound yards of tape from their legs or tore Velcro straps and removed the more compact shipping bandages; some horses side-stepped as their owners tried to saddle them.

Riders called, "Steady," "Whoa," "It's all right, Sugar," "Easy, girl." Trucks crawled through the area, growling in low gear. A horse whinnied its anxiety. More trucks with horse trailers and more horses arrived every moment.

Elizabeth parked at the edge of the parking lot near a field. The visiting riders had no stalls and used the parking lot or surrounding fields to work on their horses and the front of their trailers to store their tack. Gillian and Carley fetched the equipment they would need from the trailer and dropped it on the ground.

"No rain." Elizabeth pushed back her hair and looked at the brightening, blue sky. "A small mercy for which I am grateful."

Carley unlocked and opened the rear door while Gillian leaned through the side window and pulled the loop that tied Hawkeye's halter to the front of the trailer. Then she moved to the back of the trailer, leaned in and released the bum-strap. "Back," she said. Hawkeye obediently backed down the ramp. Gillian caught the lead rope as Hawkeye reached the ground. Years of training and practice had made his exit smooth and efficient. Gillian walked Hawkeye to the side of the trailer near the equipment and tied the lead rope to a ring on the trailer. She was working on Hawkeye's back with a brush and curry comb when Carley and Jupiter joined her.

"I'll be in the stands," Elizabeth said as she turned to leave.

"Sleeping?" Carley asked.

"Probably. Don't be so critical. I got you here. Don't expect me to stay awake as well." Her face was serious, but Gillian could see those lines at the edge of her eyes crinkle.

"You did just fine, Mom. No crashes. No falling asleep at the wheel." Carley tried to keep her face solemn.

"I know. It was pure luck that we arrived unscathed. You have no respect, my poppet. Your dad should stay home more often and cure you of irreverence. Put everything back in the trailer when you finish, and lock it." She handed the keys to Carley and left.

Gillian watched Elizabeth walk away and asked curiously, "Where is your dad? I've never seen him."

"I told you before, he's away working. He's an engineer and goes away for months at a time to foreign places to build skyscrapers and bridges and stuff."

"He comes home?"

"Sure, he comes home. But he's been away a lot in the last six months. He'll be back. He's great. You'll like him."

Gillian adjusted her ideas about Carley's home life. She had thought Elizabeth and her husband didn't like each other or were getting a divorce or something.

"Does your mom like it that way? With your dad away so much, I mean?"

"It works for us," Carley said curtly.

"Oh, sure. Great. I wasn't criticizing."

"No problem," Carley said.

For fifteen minutes the girls brushed, admired and petted their horses, then saddled them and slipped on the bridles.

"You're going to do great today, Gil."

Gillian consulted her body: shoulders tense, back sore, a lump in her stomach that felt like a nerf ball. "Sure," she said.

"No, really. This is just a fun day. No big deal."

"Yeah, a piece of cake," Gillian agreed as she snapped her black velvet hard hat under her chin and mounted Hawkeye. "It's a good thing Hawkeye knows what he's doing."

Carley mounted Jupiter and followed Gillian at a walk to the outdoor practice ring. "Come on. Loosen up."

Loosen up, Gillian thought. Right. It was easy to tell herself that, and hard to do it. Breathe deeply. Concentrate on letting warm sunshine flow through every muscle of your body. At the same time, keep your heels down, toes in, back straight, head up, hands still and squeeze with your calves. She could taste the acid from her stomach.

"You want to do a posting trot?" Carley asked.

Gillian nodded and urged Hawkeye forward.

They had circled the practice ring twice before another rider joined them. Mike Yardy on big, black Fury eased in beside Gillian.

"Your hands move with every step," he said. "Your horse won't like that. It will distract him."

Gillian's eyes flew to her hands, checking their position, and then glanced at Mike's. His were steady. They probably wouldn't move if Fury flopped onto his back and rolled over.

Carley bumped Fury with Jupiter, moving Mike out of her way.

"Let's walk," Carley said to Gillian.

Good idea, Gillian thought. She slowed to a walk and Mike trotted ahead.

"I hope he places at the bottom of the class." Carley stared at Mike's back.

"He won't." Gillian sighed. Mike always won. He knew how to ride and he had been right about her hands. They *would* move with every step Hawkeye took, and they weren't supposed to.

The novice class was first. Gillian had little time to worry about the competition before it was upon her. She thought she would be jumping with nine-year-old beginners, but she saw two middle-aged women and one short, plump man with a mustache waiting for the class to begin.

"Number twenty-one," the ring attendant called. Gillian squeezed her legs against Hawkeye and urged him forward.

When she entered the arena for the first time, she could almost imagine she was at home in Maple Ridge. The sand on the floor was the same dark grey. Swallows chirped and chittered high above in the dirty, white rafters the way they did at home. A mirror on the far wall looked like the dusty, wavy mirror in the Maple Ridge arena. This might not be too bad.

The jumps were low and arranged in a pattern that Gillian struggled to remember. The last one on the right was the first she must jump; then she had to circle around and take Hawkeye back over the one next to it, then canter diagonally to the one on the far left, circle and come back over the two jumps in the middle, circle again, then over the last one on the right.

You've got the course in your mind, Gillian, now don't think about it any more, just do it. Don't pay any attention to your stomach. You are not going to throw up. You are not!

The judge blew her whistle. Gillian squeezed her legs, placing her outside leg back. Hawkeye responded with a slow canter. They approached the first jump.

Lean forward slightly, shift your weight off your hip bones and put it in your stirrups, then up and over the fence. Good. Don't think about it, just head for the next jump. Pretend you are the only one here. No one is watching. You are by yourself sailing over hedges in a sunny field. Up and over. Beautiful. Keep a steady canter like the steady beat of music going on and on and on. Lean forward, shift your weight to the stirrups, and let Hawkeye do the work. Beautiful. Three jumps. Perfect.

"Just up and over, Hawkeye, you angel."

Hawkeye, unperturbed by what was for him a simple jump pattern, reliably took every jump.

"We're flying, Hawkeye, just flying," Gillian crooned in a low voice, almost hypnotized by the steady rhythm of Hawkeye's canter and his smooth arch over the jumps. The last jump passed beneath them and they were finished.

A burst of applause came from the stands. Gillian blinked, stood in her stirrups and looked over at the crowd. Elizabeth was standing, alternately waving her hands and clapping.

Gillian grinned. She looked back over the course and exhilaration rose until she felt as if she were three sizes bigger than usual and glowing with light. She'd done it! She'd really done it! It was wonderful.

Carley was waiting for her outside the ring. "Terrific. Congratulations!"

For once Gillian didn't say that it was all Hawkeye and she hadn't done anything remarkable. Her grin felt as if it were going to split her face. "Thanks," she said. "It was great."

3

Not Funny

Gillian rode in two more novice classes. She never recaptured the thrill of the first ride, but she managed to jump all the fences and stay on Hawkeye. During the last class, she worried about where her hands were and whether her weight was in the stirrups. She was preoccupied with details and didn't balance properly over the last jump. She lurched to the side but caught Hawkeye's mane and pulled herself back into the saddle. Not a good finish to the day.

"Forget it," Carley said as they unsaddled their horses beside the Mackenzies' truck. "You did so great the first time that the last time doesn't matter." She indicated the two ribbons tied to Gillian's saddle. "Pretty good for your first competition."

Gillian glanced at her second and sixth and then at Carley's impressive first and third. "I'd be happy with it if I hadn't messed up on the last ride."

Carley nodded. "A slave to your nerves."

"Something like that," Gillian agreed.

"You'll get over it," Carley said with her voice full of experience.

Carley started to unlock the trailer door when she noticed a note taped above the lock.

"Hey!" she said.

Gillian peered over her shoulder. She read aloud, "You need practice, Cobb. The basic idea is to stay on the horse. Get your weight forward." She shook her head angrily. "Mike!"

"How do you know it was Mike?" Carley asked curiously.

"M-I-K-E at the bottom. He signed it." Gillian pointed.

Carley tore the note from the door and read it. "He did," she said incredulously.

"I *did* stay on ... just."

"You were fantastic, Gill. Don't listen to him. Maybe he's jealous." Carley frowned.

Gillian raised her eyebrow in disbelief. "You're kidding. Jealous of me?"

"Of the attention you get," Carley explained. "He probably didn't like my mom clapping for you. He thinks *he* should get all the attention. Mr. Perfection. The 'classic' rider!"

"I don't think so," Gillian said. "Anyway, I don't think he needs a reason to be obnoxious, he was born warped." Gillian didn't care why Mike was harassing her; she just wanted him to stop.

"Forget Mike. Come on. Let's get this stuff put away." They stowed their tack in the front of the trailer. Gillian carefully hung her ribbons on a hook near her saddle. They looked bright and cheerful against the browns and blacks of the leather.

When they had secured the gear, Carley locked the door. "Mom wants to stay for another hour. She's got a commission for a series of horse pictures and she wants to sketch some scenes today."

"Really? What kind of pictures?" Gillian wanted to know.

"I don't ask too much until she's almost finished. Questions irritate her. I think it's for a children's book on competitive riding." Carley started toward the arena. "Let's eat."

Gillian hung back. "Carley, could you open the truck cab for me so I can get my sketch pad from my backpack? I'd like to draw for a while."

"Oh, boy!" Carley complained. "Two of you." But she fished in her pocket for the keys and opened the truck.

Gillian sat cross-legged on the grass and watched Hawkeye. He stood quietly, his chestnut coat shining in the sun, his darker mane accenting the smooth line of his neck. I should paint him like that, Gillian thought, with a green blanket over his back and that intelligent look in his eyes. I'd like to show how smart he is.

"Hey! Gillian!" a voice penetrated her concentration.

Gillian stared at Carley.

"I asked if you wanted me to get you a hot dog."

"Sure. Whatever." Gillian nodded.

After Carley left, Gillian began to sketch Hawkeye. She would show his size, his gentleness and his intelligence. She worked slowly, trying to get the proportions of his head and shoulders just right. She had almost finished when she heard a voice calling her. She looked up. Mike Yardy sat on Fury a short distance from her, watching. Gillian looked at him, then away. That's when she noticed a hot dog beside her on the ground. Carley must have come and gone while she was drawing. She put her pencil in her shirt pocket and picked up the hot dog. She bit into it. It was cold; she ate it anyway.

"What are you doing?" Mike asked from his position far above her.

"Drawing," she said.

"Let me see."

"No." Gillian took another bite of her hot dog.

"Hey, show me your art or I'll come down there and make you." Mike's tone was teasing, but Gillian responded to his words.

"Dumb move, Mike," Gillian said. "Fury would run away and you'd spend the rest of the day chasing him." Fury was only under control when Mike was on his back. Once he dismounted, Fury would disappear.

Gillian munched her hot dog, savouring the sweet relish and the sharp taste of mustard on her tongue. She studied Mike. He was taller than she with sandy-coloured hair, cut short. He wore the black hard hat, black riding coat and tan breeches that were the usual uniform for riders. Gillian didn't like his looks very much. Everything about him seemed pale: pale skin, pale blue eyes, pale lips. In fact, if she were going to paint him, she'd have to use a lot of white.

"So what happened to you on the last ride?" Mike leaned back in the saddle, allowing the reins to hang in a loop.

Gillian licked the last of the mustard from her fingers, wiped them on the paper napkin and fished out her pencil. "Nerves," she said. She wondered if she should draw Hawkeye's back foot again. It didn't seem to be at quite the right angle.

"So, how did you manage the first event like a pro?" Mike persisted.

"Talent," Gillian said absently. She would redraw it. She carefully erased the offending foot.

"You need to practise more. Lots more." Mike said as he leaned over Fury's mane.

Gillian started to sketch. "Go away, Mike."

Gillian worked for a few seconds before a shadow crossed her paper. She looked up to see the big horse tossing its head above her. Fury! So close! He could crash down on her, squashing her like a pop can. She scrambled to her feet and backed toward the fence. Fury with Mike on his back followed, tossing his head and almost dancing sideways, but still advancing on Gillian. Her heart raced. She swallowed. Just a few more steps. She had been slowly getting used to horses and didn't jump away from them so often now, but Fury was so big! She almost fell over the low fence in her hurry to get away. She waited on the other side, watching Mike warily. Would he put Fury over this fence? Where would she go to avoid him?

Mike gathered the reins, pulled back and brought Fury under control, backing him away from the fence. He darted a quick look at Gillian as if to make sure she was not hurt and then he laughed. "You move faster than a cornered mouse when you're scared. If there were ribbons for riders jumping fences, you'd get a first."

Gillian glared at him. She hated being afraid of horses, and she hated Mike knowing about it.

He grinned and rode away.

"Slime-ball!" she called to Mike's back. "Pond scum!" Maybe Fury had lunged forward only because Mike had held the reins so loosely, but when he'd frightened her, Mike hadn't apologized. He'd thought it was funny. Rat! Sicko!

She climbed back over the fence, retrieved her sketch pad and stared at the almost completed picture of Hawkeye. She flipped the page and quickly drew the way Fury had looked to her when she first saw him above her — all mouth and teeth and huge hooves. Then she flipped the page again and drew a cartoon of Mike, his head a pumpkin, riding a saw-horse into a ditch. Then another, this time Mike was a donkey being ridden by Fury. Then another of Mike on Fury prancing in front of a mirror in a tight circle while other riders formed a group apart from him. She was so engrossed in the anger that fuelled her drawing that she didn't hear Carley and Elizabeth approach.

"Hey!" Elizabeth said.

Gillian looked up, the anger still sparking in her eyes.

"Trouble?" Elizabeth asked.

Gillian nodded and stopped drawing.

"May I?" Elizabeth held out her hand, and Gillian slowly passed her the sketch pad.

Gillian felt her shoulders relax. "Thanks for the hot dog," she said to Carley. "How much do I owe you?"

"Buy me one next time. I hope you got it before it was cold. I didn't talk to you because you were spaced out drawing, and Mom kills me if I interrupt her."

"Yeah. Thanks," Gillian said. "I never saw or heard you, but I ate it. It's okay cold."

Elizabeth was flipping the pages of the sketch book. "These are good, Gillian. Especially the one of Mike's horse."

Gillian looked over Elizabeth's shoulder. Fury didn't seem so strong or so intimidating now that Gillian had captured him on paper. She nodded in agreement.

"These are a little ..." Elizabeth's voice died away. She tapped the picture of Mike. "I guess he annoyed you."

"He makes me sick," Gillian said.

"He makes you draw," Elizabeth corrected. "They're very clever."

"Let me see," Carley moved closer. "Hey, that *is* Mike. That really is! Oh, man." She started to laugh. "That's just like him. Crashing in where no one wants him. They're great, Gillian."

Gillian smiled. She felt better.

They talked about the competition on the way home; the jumping patterns, the problems of striding, judging the distance between jumps, arching, the position over the jump and speed. For the first time Gillian felt that perhaps she might like the competitive shows, the jumping classes and the ribbons. If she could forget about the people watching and forget about doing a perfect job, she might love it. She wanted to feel again the sense of flying that had possessed her in the first class.

"The next competition is a recognized show at our arena," Carley said, reading from a calender. "That show is a qualifier for the MacAllister Competition in Calgary. If we place well, Gillian, we could compete there."

Elizabeth groaned.

"You'll like it, Mom. You'll get to drive us through the Rockies, pay the entrance fees and feed us at all the pit stops on the way."

"What a treat." Elizabeth glanced sideways at Carley, but she was smiling.

"We have a good chance. I'm doing great, and since Gillian is competing in the novice class, she might win a chance to go too."

"All the way to Calgary?" Gillian felt her stomach cramp. She wasn't ready for bigger competitions. The Calgary show, with more people, noise and confusion, would be scary, very scary. But along with her fear, she felt something else — a shiver of excitement. "We might go?"

"Yeah, to the MacAllister Competition."

Elizabeth turned the truck into the stable driveway. "There is the small matter of earning a place first."

"We'll do that," Carley said. "I almost made it last year. This year for sure."

"Visualize success and it's yours?" her mother asked.

"Exactly," Carley agreed.

Elizabeth backed the trailer into the Maple Ridge stable yard. Carley and Gillian unloaded their horses, returned the riding gear to the tack room and left feed and water in the stalls. It was a few short blocks to Gillian's house.

"Thanks for driving me, Mrs. Mackenzie," Gillian said as they drove into her yard.

"Elizabeth," she corrected absently.

"Okay." Gillian pushed on the door handle.

"Just a minute, Gillian."

Gillian paused.

"About those drawings you did of Mike," Elizabeth began.

"Yes?"

"You can do whatever you like with them," Elizabeth said slowly, "but remember that you must use your talent to make the world better, not worse."

Gillian waited, but Elizabeth was through with her advice. Carley said nothing.

"Okay. Thanks for the ride." A little puzzled, Gillian jumped to the ground and shut the truck door.

"No problem. We'll see you next week," Elizabeth said.

Gillian watched the truck drive away. What did Elizabeth mean, Gillian shouldn't use her talent to make the world worse? She wasn't planning on hurting anyone. Mike would never see her cartoons, but she felt better for making him look silly on paper. It hadn't hurt him any. Elizabeth had liked her picture of Fury. That picture had come from Gillian's fear. The pictures of Mike had come from her anger. Why wasn't one as good as the other?

4

No Time, No Place

The big cedars in the front yard drooped over the house like protective spirits. The house was similar to the other three-bedroom family homes on the street, but the trees in the front and back yard made it seem special. Richard's bike lay in the driveway. Her mother's car sat in the car port.

The house was quiet when Gillian let herself in the back door. Her mother Margaret was marking her fourth-grade papers at the kitchen table. The noise of Richard's television show drifted in from the den. The smell of spicy sausages hung in the air, prickling the inside of her mouth.

"Your dinner's in the fridge," her mother said, pushing her hair away from her eyes. "Microwave it. There's ice cream for dessert."

Gillian nodded and dropped her backpack by the door.

"Did you have a good time?" Margaret put down her pencil and turned to her daughter.

"Yes." Gillian concentrated on the microwave dial and punched in the numbers she wanted. She waited while the machine whirred.

"And?" her mother prompted. "How did you do?"

"I won a second and a sixth," Gillian said quietly.

"Is that good?" her mother asked.

"Okay." Gillian wondered if she could tell her mother how exciting that first ride had been. She looked up in time to see her mother glance down at her work. Maybe not tonight. "What did you and Rick do today?"

"I took Richard to his soccer game. His team won," Margaret answered without looking up.

Gillian nodded. Her mom's brown hair shone in the light of the overhead lamp. Her face was in shadow but Gillian could see she had faint smudges under her eyes.

Gillian collected a knife and fork, her hot food from the microwave and stood at the kitchen counter to eat.

"You can use the table. I'll clear a space." Margaret started to rise.

"No, it's okay. I won't be long."

There was silence for a few moments while Gillian ate. The big clock over the sink ticked away long seconds. The tap dripped in an uncoordinated rhythm. Gillian looked at the pools of light, one over the sink and one over the table. The edges of the kitchen were indistinct, blurred by the coming darkness. If I painted this, Gillian thought, I'd use violet and black, maybe some green-grey.

Her mother's voice startled her. "Tomorrow I have a staff meeting. Richard will have to go with you to riding."

Gillian thought about that. Before she started riding lessons she had babysat Rick every day after school. Now he stayed at the school until her mother was ready to come home. They couldn't afford a babysitter. "Is that okay with the stables? I mean, I'll be riding. I won't be on the ground looking after him."

"He has to be somewhere!" her mother said in exasperation. "He's eight years old. Old enough to sit quietly and watch!"

Old enough, Gillian thought, but not capable. She'd never seen him still for more than one minute. He moved fast and erratically from the moment his eyes blinked open in the morning until he collapsed at night.

"Home from the horse thing?" Richard zoomed into the kitchen, flipped on the overhead light and hauled open the fridge door. "Win anything?"

"A second and a sixth."

"Yeah? Not bad." He looked back at her, his short hair, wet from his shower, standing up in a million exclamation points and emphasizing his open, curious look.

Gillian smiled at him. "You won your game, I hear. That's good. Score anything?"

"An incredible goalie-defying goal and two assists." Richard poured himself a glass of milk, spilling some on the counter.

"Any professional scouts pick you up?"

"Not this time." He grinned again and was gone.

The next day Richard walked to the stables with Gillian. He was full of questions about where the horses were and, for some reason, what they ate.

Gillian introduced him to Julie.

"I would love to have you here if you were riding, Rick." Julie spoke quickly. She didn't sound angry, just firm. "But since you are not riding, you won't be able to stay."

Gillian and Richard stared at her. Gillian saw the tilt of Julie's chin, the determination in her eyes. Richard, for once, was quiet.

Julie opened her office door and walked in. Gillian and Richard followed her. "Where is your mother right now?"

"In a staff meeting at school." Gillian answered.

Julie nodded and reached for the phone. "What is the number of the school?"

Gillian gave it to her.

Gillian heard Julie ask the school secretary to pull her mother from the staff meeting. Her mother's voice crackled in the telephone. Julie was curt. "You will have to come and remove your son, Mrs. Cobb. We don't have day-care facilities here … No, I will not keep him today. I'm not insured for it."

She hung up the phone and nodded to the door. "Gillian, you go to your lesson. Rick, you stay with me until your mother comes for you."

"You won't let me stay here?" Richard asked incredulously. "I haven't done anything."

Yet, Gillian thought. You haven't done anything yet.

"It's not your fault," Julie said to Rick and then looked at Gillian. "Go, Gillian."

She went. Julie was usually easygoing except when she thought you were doing something wrong. This was probably one of those times.

That night, when Gillian walked in the door at home she felt her mother's anger. It was like walking into a thousand icy needles prickling everywhere.

"It seems your riding is too important to have you distracted by your brother," Margaret said sarcastically.

Gillian shot a quick look at her mother's face. It was flushed. A frown crimped her forehead. Her hands were drumming on the counter. This was not going to be easy.

"I didn't know they wouldn't let kids stay there. Something about insurance."

Margaret shook her head. "You tell me how I'm supposed to pay the mortgage, put groceries on the table, pay all the soccer fees and your painting supplies and be a teacher and mother at the same time. Just tell me how that's supposed to work, okay?" Her mother's words rolled into the air like an avalanche gaining speed as she spoke.

Gillian took a deep breath and tried to speak calmly. "I didn't know that Julie wouldn't allow kids at the stables, Mom. Maybe Dad could put Rick into riding."

"Your dad is paying thousands of dollars for lessons and boarding fees for you. He's not going to pay twice. And I wish he'd pay for everything like the extra clothes and the entry fees. Do you know how hard it is to take grocery money and put it on a horse?" Her voice was still high and her words quick.

"I didn't know you paid the fees," Gillian said. Her mom had to pay the entry fees? "Maybe I should get a job."

"Riding horses is a job. You don't have time for anything else." She slammed the paring knife down on the cutting board. "I wouldn't mind," she said finally, "if I thought all this riding was going to lead somewhere. But it won't. You'll have a nice time, meet people who have ten times the income I do and generally get dissatisfied with the life I can provide. I told your dad it was not a good idea, but no, he knows best."

"But I think I like it, Mom." Gillian spoke quickly. She was amazed at how much she wanted to compete. A month ago, she might have agreed with her mother that the competitions were too much trouble and not important — but not now. She didn't know what to do or how to make her mother feel better. She had thought her dad was paying for everything: the riding lessons, the competition fees, everything.

"Of course, you like it. Who wouldn't?" Margaret continued, "but it isn't real life. You aren't really going to ride horses for a living."

Gillian said nothing. Rick wasn't going to play soccer for a living either, but her mom enrolled him and took him to practices and games. Her mother wasn't being fair. It wouldn't help to say so. Nothing Gillian could say right now would help. Silence seemed like the best plan.

"Now I have to keep him at school or pay someone to look after him," Margaret complained, "and it's all so hard!"

Still Gillian said nothing. She didn't know if her mom would do something drastic like forbid her to go riding, or something uncomfortable like send a message to her dad, or something scary like yell at her. Margaret had never hit her, but sometimes the yelling felt like hitting.

"Oh, go do your homework." The anger in her mother's voice stopped any further conversation. Margaret turned away to the carrots on the kitchen counter. "Supper will be in an hour."

Gillian escaped to her room. Through her window she could see the pink blossoms of the cherry tree in the yard. She followed the movements of one delicate branch dipping with the wind. The blossoms shivered; some fluttered to the ground. Gillian let thoughts dance around in her head.

Her mom didn't think she was going to be a good rider. She had nearly said so. Why do it? her mother had said. Almost, why waste riding lessons on you? But she *was* going to be a good rider. Gillian knew that somewhere inside her she had decided that she and Hawkeye were meant to jump. She could see herself doing it and doing it very well. She was going to be excellent. Carley believed in her. Gillian knew she could do it. No one was going to stop her. Not her mother, not Mike Yardy. No one.

5

Show Time

The next Sunday morning found Gillian at the Maple Ridge stable, carefully brushing Hawkeye, smoothing his coat and cleaning his feet.

"Stand still, baby," Gillian patted Hawkeye's shoulder and rubbed his forehead. Hawkeye butted her hand and shifted impatiently.

"Cookies." Gillian reached into a yogurt container on the ground and brought out two cubes of compressed alfalfa. "You live your life from cookie break to cookie break. I wish that was all I worried about." At least her mother and Richard wouldn't be at the show today. They had to visit Gillian's grandmother. It was Grandma's birthday.

"I can't *not* go to see Grandma," her mother had said. "She'd be hurt."

"I'm okay," Gillian had told her. "There are lots of horse shows coming up." Now she was glad her mother wasn't in the stands. It would be easier to concentrate on riding without thinking about her mother watching her.

"Here." She thrust her hand toward Hawkeye.

The horse leaned forward and with a delicate quiver of his lips located the cubes on Gillian's hand, then carefully picked them up. He munched on them, momentarily satisfied while Gillian cinched the girth, the elastic and leather strap around his belly that held the small English saddle securely in place.

Gillian left Hawkeye for a moment and darted into Jupiter's stall.

"Are you ready?" she asked Carley.

"Just about." Jupiter was saddled and bridled, but Carley was tying something onto the pommel at the front of the saddle.

"What is that?"

"My lucky crystal," Carley said.

Gillian looked closely at the tiny amethyst crystal hanging from a string. "What does it do?"

"It brings me power," Carley said, her blue eyes wide and serious.

Gillian looked at her friend steadily until Carley's eyes started to sparkle.

"You're kidding," Gillian said.

"A little." Carley patted the saddle. "Crystal for power and," she patted her jacket pocket, "lavender for luck."

"Show me," Gillian asked, curious now.

Obediently, Carley pulled out some twigs of lavender herb. "Here." She picked one from the bunch and handed it to Gillian. "Good luck."

"Thanks." Gillian carefully tucked it into her own pocket. She felt happier somehow, as if Carley's positive attitude was with her.

Carley started to lead Jupiter from the stall. "Whoops. I forgot my crop." She handed Jupiter's reins to Gillian and turned back to her tack box.

Gillian led Jupiter into the alley, staying well ahead of him and watching his front feet. When he stood quietly, she managed to pet him before Carley joined them.

Carley took the reins. "See you outside," she called over her shoulder as she led her horse away.

"I'm coming." Gillian returned to Hawkeye, grabbed her helmet and riding crop and started for the outside corral. She paused in front of the full-length mirror near the door and checked to see that her jodhpurs had no new dirt marks, her jacket had all the buttons in the correct holes and her hair was still in a tight bun inside her hair net. She snapped on her helmet and mounted.

"You ready for this, Hawkeye?" she said anxiously as she leaned over his neck and gave him a quick pat.

He shook his head and whinnied, apparently more interested than anxious.

Hawkeye loved to jump. He liked the courses, the set patterns of jumping, the complexity of managing his stride and the excitement of the shows. Some horses had to be encouraged at just the right moment or they would refuse the jump. Hawkeye never refused. He might jump before a beginning rider was ready, but he'd still jump.

Elizabeth was standing beside Carley when Gillian rode over, patting Jupiter's neck and discussing the jumping course. Carley's course was different from Gillian's because Carley rode in an age class with thirteen to sixteen-year-old riders. Gillian wouldn't have had a chance in that class, so Julie had entered her in a novice class for riders who had not won the previous year. One woman, an adult, was a natural rider who practised a lot. Gillian didn't think anyone could beat her.

Gillian looked over the yard at the trailers parked at awkward angles, the trucks and cars in haphazard rows and a mobile hot-dog stand near the entrance to the arena. This was the biggest show she had attended. Horses, vehicles and people had been arriving since eight in the morning. Twenty people, some Gillian had never seen, were competing in her class.

"Too many riders," Gillian thought. "I won't even get a sixth today."

Mike Yardy trotted up on Fury and spoke as if he had been reading her mind. "Not much chance for you today, Gillian." He looked confident and competent. Gillian's eyes narrowed. She wished he would turn purple. She wished he would lose his sandy hair until he was bald. She wished he would fall off his horse into the mud. She said, "I'll be all right."

"'All right' won't cut it. 'All right' isn't good enough."

"Mike, you are not helping me at all. You're Mr. Negative."

He stared at her for a moment. "If you listened to me, you'd get better faster. I had a lot of help when I first started. My dad hired an Olympic trainer. I had the best. It'll help."

"Do me a favour, Mike. Don't help me. Okay?"

Mike seemed frozen for a moment, then pulled the outside rein, turning Fury to one side, and rode away from Gillian.

"You'll be fine," a voice said from the ground.

Gillian looked down. Elizabeth patted Hawkeye's neck.

"Old Hawkeye knows all the jumps," Elizabeth said. "Just let him set the pace and go with him."

Gillian smiled. "Yeah, it's easy. Just keep my head up, my hands still, my heels down, my toes forward, my calves in contact with the horse and my shoulders and knees and ankles in a perfect line. Don't pull on the reins after the jump and remember to jump the fences in the right order."

Elizabeth laughed. "It will all become much easier in time."

"Thanks," Gillian said, but she didn't have a lot of time. The competition was this morning and she had to remember everything immediately.

Gillian took her place among the twenty riders waiting in single file for their turn to perform in her class. Gillian on Hawkeye was eighth, wearing a black number 81 pinned to the back of her jacket.

"I don't care about winning," she whispered to Hawkeye as she leaned forward to pet his neck. "I just want to get over the jumps without falling off, losing a stirrup or doing anything totally geeky."

Gillian reviewed the course in her mind. First, jump the blue poles on the right. Second, ride diagonally across the arena, then jump the orange one. Circle, then take the combination in the middle. Circle, then jump the green fence. Ride diagonally across the arena to the white Oxner, the double fence. Then back to the blue jump and finish. If the judge blows her whistle, indicating that she has completed the course under the set time, then she must "jump off" — take a new set of jumps: over the orange jump, then diagonally across the arena to the blue jump. Circle and over the orange. Gillian thought that was the course, but right now, she wasn't sure of it.

"We'll be all right." She spoke to Hawkeye confidently, but her hands were shaking. Her stomach cramped. This wasn't good. Winning doesn't matter, she reminded herself. Just enjoy the jumping.

She looked past the barns, at the mountains rising blue and bold into the paler north sky. I'd use phylo blue to paint those mountains, she told herself, with some black and a tinge of purple to make them seem alive. Her eyes travelled over the scene. Maybe a bit of yellow with white for the dogwood blossoms at the side of the meadow and lots of blue with a bit of yellow for the grass.

When the ring attendant called, "Number 81," she was calmer.

Hawkeye shook his head once. The judge blew her whistle, and Gillian squeezed her knees and legs, urging Hawkeye forward. She pulled Hawkeye to a stop, put her riding crop and reins in one hand, dropped the other and saluted the judge with a nod of her head. Then she gathered the reins and squeezed her calves as a signal to Hawkeye to walk. She touched him behind the girth with her outside heel. Hawkeye responded to the signal by breaking into a smooth, slow canter. After one warm-up circle at the end of the arena, they approached the starting line and the first fence in perfect rhythm. Hawkeye brought both feet together, pushed off with his hind quarters and sailed over the fence. Gillian concentrated on keeping her knees over her ankles and letting Hawkeye come back into her hands without pulling up on the reins. Perfect.

She turned toward the orange fence, which lay diagonally across the ring and was the farthest away. Hawkeye didn't seem to be approaching the fence directly. Were they going to hit the side? Just before the jump Gillian remembered to check her position. Her weight was too far back. She quickly leaned forward just as Hawkeye jumped. Her hands jerked the reins on landing. Hawkeye protested by shaking his head and prancing a little. Uh oh. That wasn't so good.

"Sorry, Hawkeye," Gillian whispered as she circled and headed for the combination jumps down the middle. Hawkeye took them easily. Gillian concentrated on keeping her weight in the correct spot. Then on the second jump she forgot to hold her hands still. Hawkeye snorted as she yanked the reins.

"Sorry, I'm really sorry, baby."

She approached the next jump, concentrating on her hands. This time she forgot her feet and almost fell into Hawkeye's neck on the landing.

Tears stung her eyes. She was not going to win. Then she stiffened. She was not even going to finish the course at this rate. She managed the next jump, remembering her feet *and* her hands. The last jump was as perfect as the first. Gillian felt relieved. She knew she had not won. Finishing the course wouldn't get her first prize, but she might get a fourth or fifth.

The judge blew her whistle. Gillian stared at her. She had completed the course under the set time. That's what the whistle meant. Now, she had to do a short jump-off pattern — and she couldn't remember it. Her mind froze. Where was she supposed to go first? Was it the orange fence on the right? The blue one? And which one after that? Hawkeye pawed with his front foot. He knew that whistle meant he could jump again, and he was ready.

Gillian had to do something. She set Hawkeye at the blue fence and sailed over it. The whistle shrilled a signal to leave the course. It had been the wrong fence. Stupid! She'd been disqualified. She bit her lip. How could she have forgotten the jump-off course? First she had jumped badly, and then she'd forgotten the jump-off course. She was a lousy rider.

She took a deep breath, held her head high, her back straight and signalled Hawkeye to trot away from the ring.

6

Confusing Times

Elizabeth was waiting for Gillian in Hawkeye's stall.
"You did well," Elizabeth said.

"No, I didn't," Gillian said bluntly as she hauled the saddle from Hawkeye's back. She picked up the curry comb.

"You did all the jumps and some of them were very good," Elizabeth offered comfort.

"Not true." Gillian glanced at her. "I thought I'd be glad if I just jumped well, you know, the way I did the first jump and the last jump of the course." She turned back to Hawkeye and brushed his coat in repeated, long strokes.

"It wasn't enough?" Elizabeth prompted.

"No, maybe not." Gillian grasped Hawkeye's mane with both hands and wove his hair between her fingers. She lay her head on her arms and turned slightly to speak to Elizabeth. "I thought it wouldn't matter if I didn't win anything. I just wanted to jump with Hawkeye. Have a good time."

"And?" Elizabeth said.

"It matters," Gillian said flatly. "I want to win."

Elizabeth smiled. "No kidding? You're becoming a competitor."

Gillian released her grip on Hawkeye's mane. "I guess so." Then she shook her head. "I can't believe I was so stupid."

"Stupid? Forgetting the jump-off course, you mean?" Elizabeth asked.

"Yeah." Of course, Gillian thought, wasn't it obvious?

Elizabeth petted Hawkeye. "You didn't expect to do well enough to *have* to jump off."

"That's right. I didn't think Hawkeye and I would move through the event so fast."

"So," Elizabeth said, "you didn't memorize the jump-off pattern. Your expectations were too low."

Gillian brushed Hawkeye with rhythmic strokes while she thought about that.

She turned, leaned her back against Hawkeye and faced Elizabeth. "So if I want to win, I have to expect it and plan for it?"

Elizabeth nodded. "Carley would say, 'Visualize success.'"

Gillian felt a sudden heat of anger rise until her head seemed on fire. Carley! Carley wouldn't have forgotten the jump-off course. Carley would have remembered it all.

"Carley succeeds," she said tightly. "Everything about Carley helps her to succeed: lessons, practice, her mom beside her. You can't compare us."

Elizabeth put her hand on Hawkeye's rump and leaned toward Gillian. "I didn't mean to compare. Carley did well, but you did too."

Gillian turned back to her grooming, glancing sideways at Elizabeth. She saw a short woman with long wavy hair, earrings dangling almost to her shoulders and no make-up on her face. She looked nothing like her own mother. Not at all like her own mother. So why was it *Carley's* mother who was standing in the stall talking about riding and not *her* mother. Gillian had a sudden notion that if she couldn't have her own mother with her, she didn't want any one.

"I did well," Gillian quoted sarcastically. "I did so well I was disqualified."

"You just forgot the jump-off course, Gillian." Elizabeth still tried to comfort her. "Don't be so hard on yourself. You were tense, so you forgot."

"You don't know what I was." Gillian tried to hold on to her temper.

"Come on," Elizabeth said. "It doesn't matter."

"It *does* matter," Gillian said vehemently, facing Elizabeth. "Don't tell me it doesn't."

Elizabeth's eyes narrowed. "I understand that it was important to you and you're disappointed. It's not the end of the world."

"Just leave me alone. Okay?" Gillian said, turning back to her grooming.

"I'm trying to bolster you, not criticize you."

"Don't do anything to me. Just leave me alone," Gillian snapped.

Elizabeth stepped back. "All right."

Gillian kept her eyes on Hawkeye as Elizabeth left. She heard the stall half-door open and close. She continued to brush Hawkeye, who had shifted a little nervously when Gillian had raised her voice. Gillian's brush strokes got slower and slower. Tears smarted in her eyes. "What a geek I am. What a dumb thing to say," she thought as she stared at Hawkeye's back. "I should have kept my mouth shut, waited and gone home to paint." She felt the rough texture of Hawkeye's hair, the warmth of his body, the solid, substantial bulk of him. "I piled stupidity on top of stupidity today." She sighed. "It's not Elizabeth's fault that she's not my mom." Gillian rubbed her cheek absently against the warmth of Hawkeye's neck. "This morning I should have asked Mom to be here today and told her I didn't want her to go to

Grandma's. I didn't even *ask* her to stay — not that she would have — but I could have asked."

Hawkeye shifted under her weight. Gillian patted him absently.

She had finished grooming Hawkeye and was spilling feed into his bucket when she heard footsteps thumping down the alleyway to her stall.

"So," Carley said as she flung open the stall door. "You smart-mouthed my mom!"

"It was nothing," Gillian said.

"You hurt her feelings," Carley insisted.

Gillian looked away. "I didn't mean to."

"'Didn't mean to,' isn't good enough," Carley said. "You did."

Gillian picked up the halter and hung it on a nail. She slipped out of the stall, waited while Carley followed her, then locked the door.

"Your mom," Gillian said carefully, "was pushing."

"My mom," Carley said with poisonous mimicry, "was trying to help."

"I don't need her help."

Carley stomped alongside Gillian as she headed for the barn door. "You need *somebody's* help."

"Hey." Mike Yardy leaned over Fury's stall door. "You sure do need somebody's help. I can't believe you blew the jump-off like that. You weren't concentrating. You've got to get it together. And your hands were all over the place."

"Shut up, Mike," Carley said. "Stay out of this."

Gillian glanced at Mike. His words reminded her that she had no friends here but Carley, and Carley was now angry.

"Look," Gillian said, trying to be cool and rational. "This is between your mom and me."

"Hah!" Carley disagreed. "It doesn't work that way. My mom and I are a team. You hurt her; you hurt me."

Gillian bit her lip. Behind Carley a few of the girls had stopped to watch the quarrel. Mike Yardy still leaned over the stall door. She could see Elizabeth in the truck at the parking lot. So many people watching. Everyone waiting. Gillian took a deep breath.

"You've got no right to talk to my mom like that," Carley insisted.

"Butt out, Carley," Gillian said quietly.

Carley straightened as if she'd been hit. "I'll do that, Gillian." Carley turned to look at the truck and then back at Gillian. "Your problem is that when you feel bad, you blame other people. It's not their fault. It's not my mom's fault that you feel bad. It's your fault. Get that right and grow up!" Then she turned quickly and ran.

7

A Win

Gillian had a week to think about what she had said and what she was going to do about it. Carley did not attend her school, so Gillian didn't see her there. At the stables, they tried to stay away from each other. They could not avoid each other for long, however. Elizabeth was supposed to haul Hawkeye to the show in Langley on Saturday.

On Saturday morning Gillian woke before daylight. She sat on her window seat and watched the gradual lightening of the sky. She saw the blurred shape of the cherry tree near the house and the bulk of the garage at the far end of the yard. Gradually light revealed the lilac hedge, the paved driveway and the fence along the road, as if a painter, starting with an undercoat of black, added colour and light to create the scene.

Gillian chased one thought through her head: she had hurt Elizabeth. She hadn't meant to hurt her; she had only been trying to make sense of her own problems. But Elizabeth had made it clear that she didn't like what Gillian had said, and Carley had made it clear that Gillian had been a jerk. Now she had no friend at the stables. Would Elizabeth be so mad that she wouldn't haul Hawkeye to the show today? If she did haul Hawkeye, would Carley sit beside her like a stone statue and say nothing for the whole trip? And why had she jumped on Elizabeth like that? It wasn't Elizabeth's fault that her mother wasn't at the show. She had to apologize. She knew she had to apologize.

Gillian hadn't had much practice at apologizing. No one in her family actually said they were sorry for anything. Usually, if her mom was sorry, she'd do something nice for Gillian or her brother, but she never talked about *why* she was sorry. And Gillian managed her hurt feelings by withdrawing and saying nothing. She often stayed in her room and painted until the anger had disappeared. That worked at home, but she knew enough about Elizabeth and Carley to realize that they would expect her to say the words.

She practised them over and over in her mind. "I'm sorry for being such a jerk." That seemed too critical of herself. "I'm sorry for hurting your feelings." What if Elizabeth said that she hadn't hurt her feelings?

Throughout breakfast, while Richard talked about his Nintendo game and her mother read the paper, Gillian thought about ways in which she could apologize. She ate very little.

"Got everything?" her mother asked her as they drove into the stable parking lot at seven o'clock.

Gillian nodded. Except courage, she thought.

"Lots of luck, then," her mother said.

"Thanks." Gillian was still preoccupied by what she had to face.

"You might wish Richard luck in his soccer game." Margaret nodded toward her brother bouncing on the back seat.

"Yeah, Rick. Slam a few in."

"No problem," he said. "Piece of cake."

Her mother waited until Elizabeth's truck drove into the yard. "Goodbye. See you tonight," Margaret said.

Gillian left her mother's car reluctantly, slammed the door and started across the parking lot. Carley leapt from the truck on the passenger side and ran for the stables. Gillian kept walking toward Elizabeth. She stopped beside the driver's door and looked up.

Elizabeth stared down at her, waiting. Gillian swallowed.

"I'm ..." She tried again. "I'm sorry." She waited.

Elizabeth nodded. "Okay."

Still Gillian waited. She realized that she was waiting for some kind of punishment.

Elizabeth opened her door. "You'd better go get Hawkeye. We have to be in Langley at nine."

Gillian spun away and ran for the stables.

All the while she was wrapping Hawkeye's legs with tape and fixing the leg pads on him, she wondered if she was finished with her apology. She didn't feel finished. She felt as if she owed Elizabeth and Carley an explanation.

She was leading Hawkeye out the barn door when she met Carley with Jupiter. They stopped and looked at each other.

"I told your mom I was sorry," Gillian said. "I am, you know."

Carley dropped her eyes for a moment. Gillian could see her take a deep breath, then she said, "My mom told me I had to apologize to you."

"You do?" Gillian was puzzled. "What for?"

"For interfering. She said you and she had a problem and it was none of my business, and that I shouldn't ... what did she say ... 'withdraw my friendship' over something that didn't concern me. Except I didn't see it like that exactly."

Gillian started to smile. "You know, Carley, that's a terrible apology."

Carley smiled back. "It's not making it?"

"Oh, I don't know. It'll do. I wasn't expecting one anyway. I thought I'd have to apologize to you."

"I think you should, but Mom doesn't." Carley reached up and petted Jupiter's nose.

Gillian reached to pet Jupiter's neck, accustomed to him now and no longer afraid of him. "I'm sorry, Carley."

"Hey." Carley looked straight at her, her eyes a little bright. "I'm sorry too."

Gillian sniffed. "Friends?"

Carley nodded. "Sure."

Hawkeye whinnied and Gillian laughed. "I guess he wants to go."

"Yeah, let's get them loaded."

The drive from Maple Ridge to Langley took half an hour. This show was similar to the Cloverdale event Gillian had attended. There was a big ring, with fences set up in an arranged pattern.

"Two-foot-six to start." Amanda, a tall, blonde sixteen-year-old experienced rider stopped to talk. "It should be all right. They'll put the jumps up for the next classes. Are you jumping two-nine?" she asked Carley.

Carley nodded.

"You'll be okay, and so will you, Gillian. Hawkeye jumps like Starlight. Remember Starlight?"

Again, Carley nodded.

"Wasn't that the horse Mike Yardy had when I first came to the stables?" Gillian asked Amanda. She remembered the horse with the beautiful name.

Amanda turned to Gillian. "That's right. Remember how she jumped eagerly, the way Hawkeye does? That sure gives the rider confidence. Not like my Peter Puck. He decides at the last minute to jump. I'm never sure if he's actually going to jump or refuse."

"Right." Gillian nodded, mentally comparing Hawkeye to Amanda's horse.

"See you later."

Amanda left and Gillian tightened the girth of her saddle, thinking about Amanda's friendliness.

She was struck with a new idea. Maybe Amanda hadn't been unfriendly before. Maybe now she talked to Gillian because now Gillian knew more about horses, and most of the conversations at the stable were about horses.

"Are you ready?" Carley asked.

"Just about." Gillian slipped the bridle over Hawkeye's head and placed the running martingale — a leather strap — around his neck, threading the reins through its rings. Hawkeye would throw his head up after the jump if she didn't use a martingale. Carley left and Gillian prepared to follow her.

"Go over each fence in your mind before the class." She heard a deep voice as she led Hawkeye from his stall. "If you want to make the Olympic team, you'll have to think like a champion."

"I know, Dad." That was Mike Yardy's voice. Gillian saw them now, Mike on Fury a few stalls away and a tall, thin man in a business suit looking up at him and giving advice.

"Keep that goal in mind. All those years of expense and hard work are going to pay off. Don't let me down, Mike."

"I won't."

Gillian led Hawkeye past Mike and Mr. Yardy. She was glad her mother wasn't standing beside her telling her she had to win. Maybe it was worse to have a parent at the stables who bossed you like that, than not to have one there at all.

Gillian picked up number 15 from the show office. Elizabeth pinned it on the back of her riding jacket. Carley had number 16.

As before, they competed in different classes. Gillian understood the competition better now and knew that she had to place in this class in order to qualify for Calgary. Carley wanted to compete in Calgary and Gillian, for the first time, thought she would like to compete in a big show as well. It was something to work for. She had a good horse. She had learned enough to do well and, if she could keep from freezing with nerves and worrying about herself, she might win a spot.

The big show in Calgary for Carley and Gillian was the MacAllister Competition, really only a small show compared to the international competition that took place the following day at Pine Valley. If they made the MacAllister Competition, they would be in Calgary to watch the international show when their own was finished. It could be an exciting weekend.

"Great competitors at the Pine Valley show," Carley had told her, "the real stars. We'd see it all."

Maybe she could take pictures of some of the competitors in action and paint them when she returned home. Elizabeth might help her with the paintings.

"Good luck," Carley said, dragging Gillian back to the present.

"Yeah." Mike Yardy moved closer until he crowded her with Fury. "Keep your mind on your jumping this time and don't stop to day-dream in the middle of the class."

Gillian flushed. She didn't think it was so obvious to others that she sometimes withdrew into another world.

"Remember, keep your hands still," Mike continued. "Don't pull back after the jump."

Gillian looked behind Mike to see if his father was still there, but he had left.

"Shut up, Mike." Carley on Jupiter pressed against Fury until Mike moved on. "Ignore him. You'll be fine."

Gillian nodded. She was the next one to compete and she needed to let Mike's words wash over her without effect. She would not think about all the things she could do wrong.

"Visualize success," Carley said. "See yourself doing it right."

Gillian concentrated on imagining herself soaring over the jump perfectly. She smiled at Carley. "Thanks."

"Go for it," Carley said.

Gillian handed her ticket to the ring attendant and urged Hawkeye forward.

The jumping course was simple this time. The orange poles, then the combination in the centre. Circle, then the combination on the left. Circle, then the orange again. All she had to do was let Hawkeye know which fence to take and he would do his best.

Gillian saluted the judge, then urged Hawkeye at a canter toward the first fence. He jumped with room to spare. Gillian remembered her hands and kept them steady, letting Hawkeye come back into position at his own pace.

They circled at that same steady canter, Hawkeye changing his lead correctly after he landed. What a beauty, Gillian thought. What a brilliant, great horse! The next two jumps looked high, but Gillian knew they were not more than two-feet, six inches. Hawkeye took them easily. Gillian smiled. They'd done it again. Two good jumps. They circled the far end of the arena at a rocking canter.

Hawkeye took the far fence and then cantered five strides diagonally across the arena to the fence nearest the judges. Again he jumped eagerly, giving Gillian enough time to place her hips and shoulders in a straight line, lean her weight into the stirrups and keep her hands steady. Another good jump.

They circled again. As before, Hawkeye changed his lead on landing, putting the correct foot forward at exactly the right time.

"Two more, Hawkeye. Let's ace this. Up and over. Come on, sweetie."

Hawkeye took the last two fences with energy and a great lift from his back feet. There was a burst of applause from the spectator stand. Gillian grinned. That felt fantastic. She patted Hawkeye. What a horse!

While she watched the others in her class compete, she tried to tell herself that it was enough that she and Hawkeye had done well; she didn't have to win a place. But she didn't convince herself because it wasn't enough. She did want to win.

"Riders in the arena, please," the ring attendant said at the end of the class. The riders entered the ring on horseback and paraded in a circle. The judge strode to the centre with her microphone. The riders stopped, all facing her.

"Thank you for such a good class," she said formally. "The first-place ribbon goes to number 43, Anne Armstrong on Miranda."

Gillian felt her stomach drop. She had wanted to be the winner so badly. Regret tasted sour in her mouth. She had thought they had done so well. "Tough, Gillian," she told herself. "That's just tough." She would not let anyone see how disappointed she was. It was probably stupid to think that she could have won. She wasn't that good.

She was so involved in mentally talking herself out of her disappointment that she didn't hear the name of the second-place winner.

"Hey," the rider next to her said. "That's you."

"Number 15," the judge repeated. "Gillian Cobb on Hawkeye."

A second! Gillian urged Hawkeye toward the judge, leaned down and received her ribbon.

"Congratulations," the judge said.

"Thank you," Gillian said soberly. Then she grinned. The judge smiled.

Gillian joined the other riders and patiently waited through the other placing awards. She noted the different shades of brown and black with splashes of white where a rider's shirt or a blaze on a black horse stood out sharply. She saw the deep black of one girl's jacket against the rich chestnut colour of her horse. She'd paint the bright red ribbons in the judge's hand and the deep blue of the fences. And somehow she'd paint the excitement of winning.

"Hey, way to go," Carley said from the side as Gillian trotted behind the string of riders leaving the ring. "Now all I have to do is win and we're on our way to Calgary."

Gillian pulled Hawkeye from the line of horses and stopped beside Carley. "Is that right? Does this second place let me move into the competition for Calgary?"

"You have two seconds in this round of regional shows. No one else has that many points."

"That's true?" she asked in amazement.

"It's true," Carley said.

"You're responsible," Gillian said. "You told me to 'visualize success.' It works."

Elizabeth was waiting near the parking lot with a video camera.

"You didn't film me, did you?" Gillian asked as she rode close to her.

Elizabeth smiled. "Yes, but I didn't tell you beforehand because I didn't want to make you nervous."

"Thanks." Gillian was glad she hadn't known.

"I just wanted to tell you congratulations. You were great."

Gillian smiled. She felt great.

"I'm going to try to get Carley on video as well. Do you need help getting Hawkeye unsaddled?"

"Are you going to help me?" Gillian teased.

Elizabeth shook her head. "No, but I'd send someone."

"You go ahead. I don't need help. I'll come when I've finished. This isn't Carley's class, is it?"

"No, the next one. You'll have time."

Gillian walked Hawkeye across the parking lot to the trailer. She unsaddled him and replaced his bridle with a halter, snapped on a lead rope and tied it to the ring on the side of the trailer. She fetched a leaf of hay and threw it down in front of him.

"You're pretty wonderful, Hawkeye." She rubbed his long nose.

Hawkeye responded by butting her hand out of his way. Gillian laughed, picked up the bridle and saddle and walked into the trailer. She had hung the saddle and was slipping the bridle over a hook when she felt the trailer dip as someone stepped in. She looked over her shoulder. Mike Yardy stood in the trailer door, a hand on either side, blocking the exit.

"I want to talk to you," he said.

Gillian turned cautiously. "About what?"

"You avoid me all the time. What's the matter? Do I have bad breath or something?" His voice seemed low and strained.

What did he want? Gillian wished she could back away from him, but there was nowhere to go. "Visualize success," Carley always said. What was success here? She wanted Mike to let her out into the sunshine. Visualize that. She closed her eyes for a second, and pictured Mike and herself outside.

"Okay, Mike. Outside."

"What?" he said, startled.

"Step back." Gillian's voice was firm.

Mike stepped back. Encouraged, Gillian took a step forward. Mike stepped back again.

"We'll talk outside." Gillian said.

"Okay," he said.

Gillian walked toward Hawkeye, relieved to have escaped from the trailer. "What's the problem?" she said.

"You don't give me the time of day," Mike complained, his voice almost a whine.

"I don't owe you the time of day." Gillian was sure of that.

Mike moved closer to Gillian until he stood on one side of Hawkeye, who had his head in the hay. Gillian stood on the other.

Mike's face was flushed now. Gillian didn't know if he was angry or hurt.

"Look, you could talk to me once in a while," he said.

"Mike, you're really pushy — and you criticize me all the time. That's why I don't want to be around you. Back off."

"Pushy? I am not! Man!" He looked bewildered. "Look, Gill. I'm in the top five percent of riders in the country. I'm headed for the Olympics in four years."

"That's nice for you." Geek! Conceited muscle head! Gillian thought. If you're so much better than anyone here, it's a wonder you even talk to us.

"I could show you how to ride better."

"No, thank you. I have Julie for that."

"You don't want my help." Mike looked as if he couldn't believe her.

Gillian looked straight at him and said clearly, "No, I don't."

"But, Gill ..." Mike stepped closer.

Gillian's hand clenched on Hawkeye's mane. He threw up his head and knocked Mike back.

"Hey, Gillian," Carley called from across the parking lot. "Are you coming to watch my class?"

"Yes," Gillian said, still looking at Mike. "I'll be right there."

Mike shook his head, turned swiftly and left.

"What was that all about?" Carley asked as Gillian walked up to stand beside her.

"I'm not sure," Gillian said, "but I don't like it very much."

8

Celebration

After the show Gillian phoned her mother from Carley's house to tell her about her second-place ribbon.

"So, was she excited?" Carley asked as Gillian hung up the phone.

"I don't know. I don't think so. She said, 'Good for you' and all that." Gillian stared at the phone for a second.

"What's the matter?" Carley said.

"She wasn't there!" Gillian burst out. "I mean, at the show. She didn't see me jump. She never watches me compete. I don't think she cares."

Carley wound a strand of her blond hair around her finger. Her eyes were serious. "Are you sure? I mean people are so different about the *way* they care."

Gillian moved toward the couch and sat down. "No, I'm not sure. I think she hopes I'll work hard and do well, but she doesn't feel bad about not seeing me."

"But mothers usually …" Carley hesitated. "I mean, she must care."

"I don't know. I don't think so." Gillian bit her lip and tried to control her tears. "She just wants me to be trouble-free. She doesn't really want to know what I'm doing or what I think."

"Are you any closer to your dad?" Carley flopped down on the sofa and picked up her cola.

"My dad's busy. We talk but … I don't expect him to watch my competitions either. He's like yours, I guess, working most of the time."

"My dad comes to my competitions when he can," Carley said, "and he knows which ones I'm in."

Gillian wasn't sure if that was true. She hadn't seen him.

At that moment the phone rang. Carley answered it.

"Hi," she said. "How are you doing?" There was silence while the person calling spoke to Carley. Then she said, "Guess what? My friend Gillian got second place in her jumping today, and I was fantastic."

Gillian listened while Carley poured out the events of the day to, as Gillian soon realized, her father.

"Mom!" Carley shouted. "Dad wants you." Carley returned to her phone conversation.

"I'll get it in here," Elizabeth yelled.

Gillian drank her cola slowly, listening to the family chatter. Carley finally wound down.

"Mom!" she yelled.

"Got it," Elizabeth answered from her studio.

Carley turned to Gillian. "That was my dad," she said unnecessarily. "He's building a bridge in Vermont."

Gillian traced the edge of her glass with her finger, round and round. "I guess my dad and yours are really different."

"Maybe," Carley said. "Want to see yourself on video?" She bounced to her feet.

"Sure," Gillian said. "Did your mom get much on tape?"

"Lots. Your class and mine, I think."

Carley tossed the remote control to Gillian, who punched the power button. Carley popped the video cassette into the VCR and joined Gillian on the sofa. Gillian heard occasional laughter from Elizabeth's studio, then she ignored it as she became enthralled by the jumping performance on the screen.

She watched her own approach to the first jump.

"Good," Carley said. "Excellent! See that? You did a perfect two-point there."

"Let me see that again."

Carley indicated the remote control. Gillian pressed the stop, rewind and play buttons. She saw herself take the first jump; her ankles, knees and shoulders in perfect alignment. The tape rolled on.

"Uh oh. See that?" Carley grabbed the remote and backed up the picture. "See how you lost your concentration when you circled? Look at your hands. They're too low. Your lower legs are good, though. It's a good thing Hawkeye wasn't upset by your hands."

"Thanks."

"Hey! No ride's perfect." She allowed the tape to run for a few seconds, then stopped it. "Look at you in this circle. Do you think you're anxious or something? You seem to tighten up."

"Maybe." Gillian stared at herself on the screen. "I think I'm more focused when we're approaching a jump. Hawkeye's terrific all the time, though."

"Yeah. He was great today."

Elizabeth joined them as Carley appeared on the screen.

"Back it up, Carley, so I can see Gillian."

Carley obediently pressed the button and ran the video back to Gillian's last jump.

"You are riding much, much better, Gillian," Elizabeth said. "Can you see that yourself?"

Gillian nodded. "Yes. It's just my hands that are so bad."

"You'll conquer that." Elizabeth motioned for Carley to freeze the picture. "Yes," she said, looking at Gillian on Hawkeye in midair, "you're getting better and you're getting competitive. That's important."

Gillian sat up straight. "I am?" She thought for a moment, then agreed. "You're right, I am."

Elizabeth laughed. "Don't sound so surprised. It would be impossible to hang around that stable and not learn to be competitive."

"Like me," Carley said.

"Like you," her mother agreed.

Carley looked away from the television, glanced at the phone and asked her mother, "When's Dad coming home?"

"Three weeks. He's thinking of joining us in Calgary if we get there."

"Right on!" Carley almost shouted.

"He wouldn't be able to drive home with us," Elizabeth continued, "but he'd be there for the show."

Carley's dad would be there for the show. Why didn't her dad come to her shows? "He has no time," she told herself. "You know that. Stop whining." She blinked and tried to smile at Carley. Carley glowed. Gillian had never seen anyone light up from the inside before, but Carley did. Her eyes grew bright, her skin seemed more alive. Warm amber, Gillian decided. I'd put some warm amber in the skin tones if I painted her.

"So how do you think you did today, Carley?" Elizabeth nodded toward the screen.

"Awesome."

They laughed.

"No, Mom. Truly. I did great. I deserved the first. See?" She ran the tape and showed her mother. "My hands are still, my heels down and my legs wrapped around the horse." She stopped the tape at the third jump. "See? This is where Jupiter got a notion *not* to jump and I had to give him more pressure with my lower legs and jiggle the reins with my inside fingers."

Gillian and Elizabeth looked hard at the tape.

"I was spectacular, wasn't I?" Carley said with satisfaction. She let the tape roll on.

"Stop!" Elizabeth cried.

Obediently, Carley stopped the tape.

"Back it up. Stop. Perfect." Elizabeth rose and approached the screen. She stared at the picture of Carley on Jupiter sailing over a jump.

"The feet," Elizabeth muttered. "I didn't get the feet right. Hold that frame while I sketch it."

Carley dropped the remote control on the couch and turned to Gillian. "Do you want another cola? Mom will be at least fifteen minutes and we won't be able to move that tape an inch until she's finished."

"What's she doing?" Gillian asked as she followed Carley to the kitchen.

"I told you. She's got a commission to do a series of paintings of horses for a kids' book. I guess she was having trouble with a jumping scene. At least, that's what I think."

Gillian looked back at Elizabeth standing in front of the television screen, her pencil flying over the paper. A studio at home and a career as a painter — maybe that future was possible for her.

9

Permission Denied

Anything's possible," Carley said as she applied Kneatsfoot oil to her saddle. "If you believe in something, it happens."

"Like magic?" Gillian asked sceptically.

Gillian and Carley were cleaning their tack, a job that they had to do every week. Gillian smoothed the oil onto her saddle and spread it evenly under the stirrup leathers, over the rough and smooth leather and into the curve under the cantle at the back. The pungent smell of the oil, the hay around them and the scent of horses in the next stall combined to create the "horse perfume" that Gillian had smelled bottled on the cosmetic counters of department stores, labelled as "Old West for Men." The real smell was richer, fuller and part of the atmosphere.

"Beliefs," Carley repeated. "If you believe you're good, you will be good."

"So, if I believe I'm beautiful, I will be beautiful?" she teased.

Carley was serious. "Yes."

"But," Gillian tried to think of a response, "that doesn't make sense."

"It does," Carley said stubbornly. "Think about it."

"If that's true, then I want to be a millionaire." Gillian was flippant.

"You can be, but you can't just *wish* for it. You have to believe it. If you believe you can be a millionaire, you will be. See yourself with all that money — pails of it, truck-loads of it." Carley drew pictures with her hand.

"Throw me a cloth, okay?" Gillian nodded at the bucket of rags beyond Carley. Carley leaned over, picked up a rag and threw it to her. Gillian rubbed back and forth, bringing out the shine of the black leather saddle.

"Do you really think that all I have to do is tell myself I am good and I'll win my class?" she asked Carley.

"Of course," Carley said confidently. "But you have to practise too. I mean you have to work at it one step at a time. It's a process, you know. Achieving is a process. First you have to believe; then you have to do."

"I can't just wish for it?"

"Too easy." Carley polished her saddle, slipping the rag over the smooth leather until she achieved a dull shine. "We're both going to Calgary. Hold on to that thought."

They spent every day during the next week at the barns, practising on the jump course with their horses, watching each other and reviewing their techniques.

Julie, encouraged by their interest, gave them more instruction time than usual and offered suggestions. "Your hands are improving, Gillian. Just remember to hold them still and lean forward slightly during the jump. Hawkeye jumps from the base. That's a good quality; go with it. Carley, Jupiter jumps late."

"I know. I know," Carley said as she brought Jupiter to a halt in front of Julie.

It was evening, still light, but darkness would come soon. Carley and Gillian were the last riders at the stables. Julie was preparing to leave.

"Come on, you two. You're almost sleeping here. You're as bad as Mike."

Gillian was curious. "Does Mike spend a lot of time practising?"

"Sure. You don't think he got that good without practising, do you?"

"I never thought about it, about how much time he'd have to spend here, I mean."

"Believe me, perfection takes practice. But you two have had enough for today. Go home."

Carley headed toward the stalls. Gillian followed. They unsaddled their horses, replaced their tack and called a goodnight to Julie as she was leaving her office. Gillian breathed in the mixed scents of horse, hay and leather. She loved the stable.

"One more win for both of you and you're on your way to Calgary," Julie encouraged.

"We'll win this weekend," Carley said.

Gillian nodded her agreement.

"Four of you from here might make it." Julie walked with them to the parking lot. "Mike Yardy should win this weekend and Alexandria shows promise."

"My mom will drive us," Carley said. "She's getting ready."

Julie laughed. "With that kind of confidence, you'll make it. Just remember to win this weekend. Then you can go."

"No problem," Carley said.

They waved to Julie and started up the road, parting at the corner, Carley going a half block to her house and Gillian another block to hers.

Her mother and Richard were both home. Richard was, as usual, in front of the television, and her mother, as usual, in the kitchen.

"Was it a good practice?" Margaret said.

"Yeah. Really good," Gillian answered. "Julie stayed and gave us some extra coaching."

"How much will that cost?" Margaret said sharply.

"Uh ... nothing. At least, I don't think so ..." Gillian's voice died away. She hadn't thought of paying for tonight's instruction. "Did Julie charge you extra last week?"

"No. Just the entry fees for the shows."

"Then she's not charging because she gave us extra time last week too," Gillian said, relieved.

"That's good." Her mother finished packing Richard's school lunch and poured herself a cup of coffee. "Is this weekend the last competition?"

Gillian brightened. "Until Calgary. If I win this one with a first, second or third, I qualify for the MacAllister Competition in two weeks. Carley has to win her class, but she will. Her mom's going to drive us. I hope Hawkeye likes to travel because it's going to be a long trip."

Margaret sank into a chair opposite Gillian. "Calgary? Why didn't I know about Calgary?"

"I told you," Gillian said.

Margaret shook her head. "Oh, no you didn't. And you're not going to Calgary."

"Mom!" Gillian felt a constriction in her throat. She hadn't thought her mom might object. Not once had she thought of it. Her mom was not going to let her go. When Margaret said no, she stayed with no. This couldn't be happening.

"Mom," Gillian tried again for a reasonable tone. "If I get enough points in all the competitions, I get to be the 'most promising novice' and that means I get to go to Calgary."

Margaret's face softened. "It's wonderful that you are doing so well, but I can't afford to send you to Calgary — entry fees, travel money, horse boarding costs, plus your share of the gas. No. Not on, kid. Sorry. I've car insurance to pay."

"Dad?" Gillian said weakly.

Margaret's voice hardened. "Your dad is paying enough. I won't ask him for more. And you are not to ask him either!"

"But, Mom!"

"Listen, Gillian. You're old enough to realize that we don't have money for all those extra treats that the rich take for granted." Margaret spoke fiercely. "It's all I can do to keep up the mortgage payments, pay the orthodontist and the house and car insurance. Other than eating, we don't have luxuries." She smiled. But Gillian saw no humour in the situation. This was devastating.

"It's not fair," Gillian said. "Why am I competing if I can't go to Calgary? Am I supposed to stop trying now?"

Margaret shrugged. "No one expected you to do so well."

Somehow, that was the worst thing she could hear. Gillian stood abruptly. She heard her mother say, "Sorry, pet. It isn't on," as she left the room.

You're not important. Your ambitions don't count. The hurtful messages pounded through her brain like a rap tape. She stared out her bedroom window seeing nothing, listening to her thoughts. What good are beliefs? She had believed she could win, but her mother hadn't, so why was her mother allowed to stomp on her dreams?

"That's a real bummer," Carley said the next afternoon. They had finished early at the stables and retreated to Carley's house to talk about Margaret's edict. "Just no?" Carley said. "Like no compromise, option or choice?"

"Just no," Gillian said. "And she's sorry about it, but no."

"Do you think she understands what this means to you?" Carley asked.

"She understands," Gillian said bitterly. "She just doesn't care."

Elizabeth walked into the kitchen and poured herself a cup of herbal tea. She looked thoughtfully at the girls, who were sitting at the kitchen table slumped over their school books.

"Bad news?" she asked.

"Gillian's mom won't let her go to Calgary," Carley informed her. "That's such a bummer."

Elizabeth put her cup on the table and drew up a chair. "Why not?"

"Too expensive," Gillian said.

"Oh." There was silence for a few moments.

"Uh. Forgive me for being nosy," Elizabeth said, "but doesn't your dad pay your bills at the stable?"

Gillian sat with her chin in her hands, staring at the table top. "Dad pays most of the bills. Mom pays the extras."

"Like entry fees?" Elizabeth asked.

"Yeah," Gillian confirmed, "like entry fees."

"Is there any other place you could get the entry fees?"

"And travel money," Gillian said, "and horse-boarding fees and my share of the gas." She quoted her mother.

"Gas is not a problem. I have to haul Jupiter anyway. But entry fees." She was quiet.

Carley leaned forward. "Don't you have a great aunt who's rich and loves you? An older uncle who's mad about horses? A millionaire you saved from certain death? Or a saddle company that wants to support your career?" Carley threw her ideas into the air one after another as if she believed that among so many there must be one that would work.

"I think," Gillian said, rousing herself from her dejection and taking an interest in investigating the problem, "that Dad might pay. Mom just doesn't want to ask him."

"And she doesn't want you to ask him?" Elizabeth guessed.

"Right," Gillian confirmed.

There was another silence.

"Well," Elizabeth said quietly, "would she object if Julie asked him?"

Gillian stared at Elizabeth. "You mean, if Julie just sent him a bill or invoice or something for the fees?"

"Yes. Or phoned to ask him if he wanted you to go."

"Yeah," Carley said excitedly. "And she could say how great you were and …"

"Competitive," Gillian said. "That would make Dad want to support me. Competitive. She should use that word."

"So … perhaps if I spoke to Julie …?" Elizabeth suggested.

"Do you think she'd cooperate?" Gillian asked, suddenly doubtful.

"Sure, why not?" Carley said. "She wants you to go to Calgary."

The clock ticked into the silence while they thought about the scheme.

"It might work," Gillian whispered.

"Believe it," Carley said fiercely.

10

On the Road

Gillian and Carley sang at the top of their voices, the sound reverberating in the cab of the truck, shaking the dust from the corners and rattling the windows.

"Peace," Elizabeth said, wincing as a particularly high note assaulted her ears. "If I have to spend the next two days with you, keep the decibels down."

Carley grinned. "No problem. No problem. We need you in good shape. I could drive this rig, of course, but there are laws against it."

"I couldn't be more grateful," her mother said solemnly.

"How long will it take to get there?" Gillian looked out the window at the tops of the trees and the valley below them. They were climbing slowly up the long ascent of the Coquihalla Highway on the first part of their trip to Calgary.

"Ages," Carley answered.

When Gillian's dad learned that she had qualified for the MacAllister Competition, he had been happy to pay her entrance fees and the expenses of the competition.

"Way to go, kid," he'd said. "I knew you'd find you were tough."

Her mother had been tight-lipped, but hadn't forbidden her the trip. She had even helped her pack and wished her luck.

"Did you make sure the hay nets were tied securely so the horses can eat while they're travelling?" Gillian asked Carley worriedly.

"They're strapped tight. Nothing is hanging down that could slap their faces. Their legs are wrapped in shipping bandages and they are comfortable. Trust me."

Gillian glanced back at the horse trailer. "Okay. Just this once."

"We'll stop at Kamloops for a tea break," Elizabeth said. "Check them out then. You'll feel better."

"Thanks," Gillian said. "Hawkeye might get tired standing and swaying for so long."

"What's your plan?" Elizabeth asked them.

"A trailer check at Kamloops," Carley said. "Then we need a complete out-of-trailer experience two hours later."

"Get the map out, Carley. Be specific," Elizabeth directed.

Carley took the map from the glove compartment and spread it over her lap and Gillian's. Together the girls planned where they would stop to give their horses exercise and water breaks.

"We'll have a long drive today," Elizabeth said, "because I'm trying to make it to Revelstoke. Aunt Marta has offered us room in her corrals for the night."

"I thought you couldn't stand her." Carley kept her finger on the route and looked at her mother curiously.

"We're civil to one another," Elizabeth said. "She's my sister. We're long past the hair-pulling and yelling stage, but I don't have to like her."

Carley turned back to the map. "It looks like we might make it there at about eight o'clock."

Elizabeth nodded. "That's why we left so early this morning. It will be a long, slow trip, the tedium enlivened only by your fascinating chatter."

"Something more to be grateful for," Carley said.

The truck and trailer headed for the Rocky Mountains on the Trans Canada route. The lush green of the Coast gave way to the dry hills of the Interior.

"The air smells clean," Gillian said as she climbed down from the truck at a Kamloops gas station.

"Not so much pollution here, although I think they have a pulp mill that can give you a pretty heady smell on a windy day." Elizabeth handed Gillian the keys to the trailer. "I'm going to the ladies room. See you in the café."

Gillian and Carley turned to check on their horses.

From the side of the trailer through the small escape door Gillian could touch Hawkeye and check his comfort without having to open the back doors or climb into the trailer with him. Hawkeye, a veteran of many trips, nickered softly and jerked his head as if to tell Gillian that, while it wasn't his favourite place, he was comfortable. His skull cap of leather reinforced with hard plastic looked like a cartoon baseball cap with spaces for his ears. Jupiter wore a similar one to protect his head if he should rear. They both wore light fly sheets over their backs and shipping bandages, thick padding secured with Velcro, around their legs. Jupiter stretched toward Carley.

"Cookies," Carley said. "He wants cookies."

"Could we feed them a couple?" Gillian asked.

"Sure. They can eat and travel. Next stop you get to exercise, guys."

Gillian filled a bucket of water in the washroom and carried it back to the trailer. She added a bottle of electrolyte solution containing potassium and sodium so that the horses would drink the strange water. She poured a half bucket of the treated water into each pail and leaned in the escape hatch to set it in front of them. She watched while they drank.

Carley carefully locked the trailer before they joined Elizabeth at the café counter.

"Juice?" Elizabeth asked. "Pop? Herbal tea?"

They settled for a soda and drank it outside where they could watch the trailer.

"We'll stop outside Salmon Arm to exercise the horses," Elizabeth said as she climbed into the truck, "and it will be clean-up time with the horses out of the trailer and exercised in as much space as we can find."

"That's about an hour or an hour and a half," Carley said, consulting her map.

They drove through the small town of Salmon Arm with its huge cottonwood trees on either side of the road and its mixture of houses, businesses and fields. On the east side Elizabeth spotted a rest stop with an adjacent park.

She pulled into the parking lot and drove under one of the cottonwood trees. By now, the sun was high in the sky and hot.

Gillian and Carley opened the back doors of the truck and pulled down the ramp. They didn't bother to open the side escape hatch, but leaned through the window and untied the lead ropes. Hawkeye backed down the ramp first and Gillian caught his halter rope. Carley released Jupiter and caught his rope.

Dust flew into the air as Hawkeye shook himself, quivering from his nose to his tail as if to shake off the enclosed feeling of the trailer.

Gillian waited. "Feeling better, Hawkeye?" She patted his neck, then led him into the shade of the trees. There was no one else in the park so Gillian and Carley ran with their horses along the path, encouraging them into a slow trot.

"Fifteen minutes," Carley called.

"Okay." Gillian jogged ahead along a path through the trees. The sun filtered through the leaves, creating dappled light and shadow on the path. Green, Gillian thought. I'd paint an undercoat of yellow-green, then add the browns of the bark and the deep green of the leaves. The horses' hooves thudded into the soft ground.

"How much more time?" Carley called.

Gillian checked her watch. "Five minutes."

"Let's head back now."

Gillian slowed to a walk. Hawkeye changed pace easily. Gillian turned and followed Carley back to the parking lot.

Elizabeth was sitting under a tree sketching the horse trailer.

"With all this great, green landscape around you," Carley complained, "why are you drawing the horse trailer?"

"I need it for the last scene in the book," Elizabeth said without looking up.

Gillian and Carley tied their horses to a fence post under a tree. From the front of the trailer they grabbed a fork, a shovel and the "dung bucket," a hard plastic container with handles on either side. They headed back into the trees to scoop up the horse manure and drop it into the bucket. In the shade of the trees the horses twitched their tails to keep the flies away from their backs and stamped their front feet occasionally to shake them from their legs.

It was while Gillian was shovelling out the horse trailer and Carley was holding the bucket that she heard Elizabeth shout, "Gillian! Your horse is loose!"

Gillian dropped the shovel and darted from the trailer. She looked over to where she had left Hawkeye in time to see his haunches disappearing into the wood. An eighteen-wheeler swooshed by on the highway.

Could Hawkeye get onto the highway from the park? She ran after him.

"Cookies," Carley said and dashed to the front of the trailer for the horse treats.

Hadn't she tied the knot in the rope tight enough? Had Hawkeye pulled it loose? Where could he go in this park?

Could he get out of it? Gillian looked around her at the acres and acres of forested land that could hide a horse for months.

"Hawkeye!" she called. "Come back here!"

Carley shoved some horse cookies toward her. "He might come for these."

Gillian could see Hawkeye disappearing down the path into the park. They ran after him. As they got closer, Hawkeye began to trot.

"Oh, no!" Carley said. "I can't outrun a horse. If he starts to gallop, we'll lose him."

The faster Gillian ran, the faster Hawkeye seemed to run. Suddenly, Gillian stopped. Carley faltered and looked at her for direction.

"Whoa!" Gillian yelled.

Hawkeye stopped.

"Stay here," Gillian hissed at Carley and slowly walked toward Hawkeye, talking softly. "That's a boy. Take it easy. I'm right here. You aren't going anywhere."

When she was close, she put her hand on his back and slid it up toward his neck. She kept one hand on his neck while she reached out with the other to present him with the cookies.

He stretched his nose toward her hand and delicately nibbled the cookies with his lips.

"Got him," Gillian said triumphantly as she dropped her hand from his neck to the lead rope.

"Excellent," Carley said. "I'm in no shape to race a horse. It's hot. I'm exhausted."

Sweat poured down Gillian's face, but she hardly noticed it.

"Don't do that again, Hawkeye, my friend," she said, rubbing his nose. "I don't want to lose you."

They returned to find Elizabeth anxiously watching the trail.

"Good," she said, her frown disappearing when she saw them with Hawkeye. "I didn't want to spend two days chasing a horse through the hills. Is he all right?"

"Sure," Gillian said. "He didn't go far." She spoke calmly, but her heart was still tripping double time. She didn't want to think about what could have happened if he had broken out of the park and into the wilderness around them.

"It was far enough." Carley wiped her face with her T-shirt. "I'm melting."

"Finish your shovelling, get the horses loaded and I'll stop at the next fast-food joint for pop."

With that promise the girls cleaned the trailer and secured their horses in quick time.

It was evening when they drove through Revelstoke. The rays of the sun lit the tops of the granite mountains with flashes of amber light that blinked out into grey. By eight-thirty they arrived at Elizabeth's sister's place east of Revelstoke. Like most houses in this area, it lay at the base of a mountain.

Gillian checked the corral poles to make sure the horses were safely enclosed and watched them roll in the dust, then take long drinks of treated water.

Elizabeth joined Gillian at the corral. Behind them a mountain rose like a rock tower. It was almost dark now and the air was cool.

"Nice to have both of them safe," Elizabeth commented.

"That was awful," Gillian said. "I thought Hawkeye might take off into the hills and I'd never see him again."

"Could have happened," Elizabeth agreed.

Gillian turned to look at her. "That isn't very comforting."

"True, though." Elizabeth's voice was calm. "It's sometimes difficult to be responsible but it doesn't help to pretend that you aren't. If Hawkeye had been lost, it would have been your fault, and that would have been hard for you."

"I don't think I could have stood it. He wouldn't know how to manage in the wilderness. He'd have been so ... so ..." Gillian searched her mind for the words to express herself.

"Vulnerable? Unsafe? Scared?" Elizabeth supplied.

"All that. He depends on me."

"Well," Elizabeth said briskly. "He isn't lost. He's right here. Don't worry about what didn't happen. He got away; you got him back. End of problem."

Gillian watched Hawkeye stomp his feet, causing clouds of dust to billow around him. "Thanks."

"Okay?" Elizabeth insisted.

Gillian smiled at her. "Okay. Everything's okay."

11

Hawkeye's Problem

They left early in the morning to drive through the Rockies on the Rogers Pass. Steep, blue mountains rose on either side, but the highway climbed and dropped in easy slopes. Its double lanes allowed the slow-moving truck and trailer to travel without impeding traffic.

"I hate two-lane roads where I look in the side mirrors and see eight cars behind me trying to find a place to pass. This is much easier." Elizabeth checked the mirrors as she spoke. "I may be only a little below the speed limit, but most maniacs drive a little above it."

They were passing through the Banff area. Soaring mountains on either side enclosed the wide valley.

"So much blue," Gillian said. "Blue sky, blue mountains, even the highway looks blue-black."

Elizabeth nodded. "It would be a challenge to paint. The result might not look real."

"Too one-dimensional?" Gillian asked, interested in Elizabeth's professional view.

"It might look like that on canvas. Not enough vitality. If I tried to paint this the way it is, you wouldn't like it. *I* wouldn't like it anyway. Too dull, too stereotypical. I'd have to add my own ideas: highlight a rock in the foreground, add light to a tree stump. Something."

Gillian looked at the spectacular mountains with new eyes, mentally changing what she saw, adding highlights and shadows.

At Canmore, on the Alberta side of the mountains, Elizabeth pulled into a rest stop for another horse check.

Jupiter seemed quiet and resigned to the long hours of standing in the trailer, but Hawkeye was restless.

He nudged Gillian's hand forcibly and shook his head free when she tried to pet him. He sniffed the water when Gillian offered him the bucket, but didn't drink.

"What do you think, Carley?" Gillian asked for a consultation. "Is he okay?"

Carley looked at Hawkeye's eyes and felt his nose. "Take it easy, Hawkeye. We're almost there." She patted his neck comfortingly. "It's hard to say, Gillian. Maybe he's just bored. He'll feel better when he's free of the trailer."

"I hope so," Gillian said worriedly.

They arrived at the MacAllister stables before supper. A stable hand showed them to the corrals.

"Hey, they have a shelter." Carley surveyed the temporary home. A shed with a roof was built into the far fence. A manger and water trough were nearby and a salt block lay on the ground under the shelter. Several horses stood around the water trough, idly swishing their tails and nudging each other.

"Comfy," Carley said. "Nice sawdust so we won't have to wash them three times a day."

"Hawkeye would rather have dirt." Gillian knew Hawkeye liked to roll in fine dust.

"Just be glad it's sawdust," Carley said. "Hawkeye is a big horse to wash."

Hawkeye backed down the ramp without trouble. Carley led Jupiter and threaded her way between the horses to the water trough. Gillian followed, telling herself that the other horses looked calm and were not going to kick or bite.

Hawkeye stretched his neck, sniffed the water, but didn't drink. Gillian left him with Carley and fetched a bottle of electrolytes and a bucket from the trailer, filled the bucket with water, added the electrolytes and set it down in front of her horse. She stood back. Hawkeye cautiously sniffed, waited a moment, then took a tentative sip.

Come on, Gillian said to herself. Drink. You'll be sick if you don't drink.

Hawkeye took another small sip, and then a big one.

Gillian turned away, relieved. He would be fine.

But later that evening after Elizabeth, Carley and Gillian had registered in their hotel, Elizabeth took a call from the stable manager. Hawkeye seemed listless. They had transferred him to a stall inside the barn. They would appreciate it if the owner would attend her horse.

The drive to the stables took five minutes. Gillian sat tense and worried, wondering if Hawkeye had influenza, pneumonia or some horrible disease she'd never heard of.

The stable manager was waiting for them and escorted Gillian to Hawkeye.

"Here," the young woman said. "Stall number 43. He may be just tired from the trip, but we didn't like the way he seemed so lethargic. Would you like me to call the vet?"

Gillian turned to Elizabeth. She *must* have the vet check him. What if something was really wrong? But how would she pay the vet?

"Go ahead," Elizabeth said, correctly interpreting Gillian's worry. "We'll settle the money later."

Gillian nodded at the stable manager who left quickly. In ten minutes the veterinarian arrived, a young man who seemed cheerfully optimistic as he approached Hawkeye.

"A little under the weather, are we?" He checked Hawkeye's heart and lungs with his stethoscope.

"Not pneumonia, anyway," he said brightly. "No nasal discharge or eye discharge so it's probably not the flu. What's the matter, fella?"

Gillian stood by Hawkeye's head while the vet ran his hands over Hawkeye's legs, then took his temperature.

"A little elevated, but nothing significant." He patted Hawkeye on the back. "I think he's emotionally upset."

"What?" Elizabeth asked. "A horse?"

"It's entirely possible," the vet said. "He may be frustrated with being cooped up for so long. Frustration could have turned to depression, and listlessness may be the way he's dealing with it."

Gillian could barely understand this. Neither could Elizabeth.

"You mean a horse could be emotionally upset? Depressed?" Elizabeth asked.

"Plenty of people are," the vet said defensively, "and people cry when they're depressed, or shout or swear. Horses do other things. Emotions are powerful, you know."

"Certainly," Elizabeth agreed. "Emotions can be strong. I believe you. I just didn't think a horse —"

"They are quite evolutionarily sophisticated," the vet snapped.

"Really?" Elizabeth raised her eyebrows, looking as if she didn't believe a word of it.

The vet ignored Elizabeth and turned to Gillian. "You might trot him up and down the alley here about three times in the night. If he exercises and sees and smells other horses, he might feel more comfortable."

Gillian nodded. "I'll do that."

"Good," the vet said. "He ought to be fine, but if he gets worse call me again. I'm on duty tonight so I'll be around." He wrote out a bill and slapped it into Gillian's hand. "Pay at the stable manager's office when you pay your stable bill."

"Thanks."

The vet closed his black bag, shoved his stethoscope into his shirt pocket and left.

Gillian stared at the bill. Fifty dollars. She handed it to Elizabeth and asked, "What about the stable bills?"

"Don't worry about them. I'll pay them and get the money from your dad. He'll understand."

Her dad might understand, but her mother certainly wouldn't.

"Now," Elizabeth said, "did you or did you not believe that amazing veterinarian when he diagnosed your horse with depression?"

Gillian thought for a moment. "Yes," she said slowly, "I think he might be right."

"A horse with an emotional illness? Too much. This is really too much." Elizabeth shook her head. "Is Hawkeye going to need tender loving care all night?"

"He might. It might be really important to him to have company tonight." Gillian added quickly, "And he's my horse. So it's up to me. Anyway, I wouldn't be able to sleep at the motel knowing he needed me."

"I can understand how you feel, but," Elizabeth looked around the stall, "I don't think ..."

"Honestly, Elizabeth," Gillian interrupted hurriedly, "I'll be fine here. I won't be alone. There will be people around all night." For a few seconds Gillian held her breath. She *couldn't* leave Hawkeye alone. Why did she have to wait for Elizabeth's permission? It wasn't fair. She knew what Hawkeye needed; Elizabeth didn't.

Elizabeth frowned. "I don't know. What is your mother going to think?"

"I'll call her," Gillian promised. "It will be fine."

"What am I supposed to do?" Elizabeth bit her lower lip. "I do see you can't leave Hawkeye ..."

Gillian waited, afraid to say anything more.

"Okay," Elizabeth said reluctantly, "I'll speak to the stable manager, but you are *not* staying unless someone can watch over you. I suppose the horses are too valuable to be left unprotected, so there should be a security guard."

"Thanks, Elizabeth." Gillian let out a long sigh of relief. "I'm supposed to exercise Hawkeye in the night," she explained. "And, anyway, I don't want to leave him."

"Not if he's emotionally distraught," Elizabeth agreed solemnly.

"It's not funny, Mom," Carley said. "He needs to be petted a lot. The vet might be right. Maybe he's just feeling depressed."

"He needs me, whatever is making him sick," Gillian insisted.

"Short of kidnapping you, I don't suppose I could get you to the motel. You can stop the heavy pressure; I'll arrange for you to stay." Elizabeth left.

Carley and Gillian remained with Hawkeye, petting him and talking to him in soothing voices. When Elizabeth returned, she brought the stable manager with her, and Gillian's sleeping bag with some supplies.

"I suggest you put a sleeping bag in the manger," the stable manager said. "If you put hay under it, it will be comfortable and you'll be protected by boards so your horse won't accidentally roll on you."

"Please do that," Elizabeth said. "I couldn't explain that one to your parents."

"Good idea." Carley helped Gillian fill the manger with hay and spread out her sleeping bag.

"And speaking of parents," Elizabeth said, "I tried to phone your mom to tell her about your sleeping arrangements, but she wasn't home."

"I'll phone her later," Gillian said quickly. "It will be all right."

"Yes. Probably." Elizabeth handed Gillian her jacket, a pair of sweat pants, a sweater, two cans of juice and her grooming equipment. Carley handed her a sprig of lavender.

"Good luck," she said.

Gillian tucked the lavender into her shirt pocket. "Thanks."

"We'll be back in the morning to pick you up for breakfast," Elizabeth instructed. "Hawkeye should be better by then. There's a phone at the end of the alley, so you can phone us if you need anything."

"The security guard, Fred, checks the stables routinely," the manager reassured her, "so you won't be alone here. I'll be around in an hour to make a check and dim the lights. We don't shut them off completely because there are still people arriving with their horses, and others like you want to spend the night in the stalls. Okay?"

Gillian nodded. She'd be fine. Hawkeye might not be, though.

Fred arrived a few minutes after everyone left and introduced himself. He was a small, wiry, old man with grey curly hair and sharp blue eyes.

"Need anything, Miss?" he asked.

"No thanks. I'm all right," Gillian said.

"Okay," Fred said. "My office is at the end of this alley. I can hear you if you yell."

Gillian petted Hawkeye and brushed him, crooning encouragement. Hawkeye stood quietly and accepted her attention but hung his head as if he was very tired. Gillian snapped a lead rope onto his halter and led him into the alley. She walked him up and back, then urged him into a trot. Hawkeye responded obediently, but slowly. After three times up and back in the alley Gillian returned him to stall number 43. By then the stable was dim, with only a few lights at the end of the alleys giving a soft glow to the huge barn. Gillian could hear horses stomp the ground and rustle hay as they ate. It was almost dark, but not frightening. She secured the door and left Hawkeye in the stall. Then she walked to the phone and reversed the charges to home.

"What's the matter, Gillian? It's late. Are you all right?" Her mother's voice held an edge of concern.

"I'm all right," Gillian said. "It's Hawkeye." She twisted the lavender between her fingers.

"Oh." There was silence for a moment, then Margaret asked, "What's the matter with him?"

Gillian poured out Hawkeye's problems, what the vet had said and what she was doing for the horse.

"Are you safe in that stable?" her mother asked sharply.

Gillian told her mother about the security guard, the stable manager and the nearby phone.

"So you're worried," her mother said, less concerned now about Gillian.

"Yes," Gillian answered honestly.

"About jumping tomorrow, or about Hawkeye being sick?" Margaret asked.

"About Hawkeye. What if he's really sick? I wouldn't know what to do for him. I wish you were here." Gillian couldn't believe she'd said that. Her statement seemed to hang on the telephone line.

There was a long silence before Margaret responded. "I don't know what I could do, Gill. I don't know anything about horses."

Once she had asked her mother for help, it seemed easier to continue. "You know about me, though. You could help me."

"I … I'm not sure I could help you. I'm not sure I really …" her mother hesitated.

"Mom," Gillian said with sudden decision, "why don't you support my riding? You don't like me doing it, do you?"

Her mother gave a long sigh. "It's not your riding I object to, Gillian. It's having to ask your dad for the money for it." She paused, then continued. "I guess I'm jealous in a way too. I get to supply you with the ordinary things like food, housing and clothes, and your dad gets to supply the glamorous stuff like riding lessons and this great trip to Calgary."

"That bothers you?" Gillian pressed the phone to her ear, concentrating on what her mother was saying.

"Yes, it bothers me. I'm losing control of everything in this family. You decide you want something like this trip to Calgary, and the next thing I know, you're going. I'm not even involved in the decision."

"But," Gillian said slowly, "you didn't want me to go."

"That's what I said, wasn't it," Margaret admitted.

"Yes."

When her mother spoke again, she sounded pensive, as if it was the first time she had considered the problem. "Truly, it wasn't so much that I didn't want you to ride in Calgary. In fact, I'm really proud of what you've done this spring with your riding. You're amazing. Really. It's just that I didn't want to ask your dad for more money." She sighed. "I'm sorry about it all, Gillian. It wasn't your fault, and I guess I wasn't being fair, worrying more about how I felt than about how you felt. It's just that there's so much pressure on me ... and ..."

"It's okay, Mom," Gillian interrupted.

"It isn't okay, really," Margaret said. "I'm sorry I made it more difficult for you."

Gillian was quiet. It was the first time she had ever heard her mother apologize. Maybe things could change. "Maybe ..." she began, then she thought for a few seconds, "maybe I should deal straight with Dad myself about riding. I mean there isn't any reason why you should have to ask him for the money, is there?"

"Well, I'm not sure you should ask him. He might give you stuff you don't need."

Gillian laughed. "Hey, Mom. Trust me a little. Anyway, Dad's not that easy a person to get money from."

"That's true," her mother said dryly.

"So trust me to decide what I need most and to ask for it."

"I guess you'll do that anyway, won't you?" her mother said.

"Probably."

"What about your horse?" Margaret reminded Gillian why she had called.

Gillian talked about Hawkeye for a few minutes and then said goodbye.

"Good luck, tomorrow," her mother said.

"Thanks, Mom."

Gillian hung up the phone and returned to stall 43. She felt better, more confident somehow about Hawkeye and about her own capabilities. Hawkeye was lying on the saw-dust floor, but lifted his head when she opened and closed the door.

"You get some sleep," Gillian said as she sank to her knees beside him and stroked his shoulder. Hawkeye allowed his head to flop back down.

Gillian roused Hawkeye twice more in the night for a walk and trot in the alleyway. Fred poked his head in a few times. He didn't stay but waved to let her know she wasn't alone. Gillian brushed, petted and stroked Hawkeye, telling him he was wonderful, healthy and strong. He seemed brighter on the last walk and even objected to going back into the stall. That seemed an improvement, so Gillian crawled into her sleeping bag in the manger and tried to get a few hours sleep.

Elizabeth's voice woke her in the morning. Gillian peered through the slats of the manger to see Elizabeth and Carley watching the vet examine Hawkeye, who snorted at him and stamped his feet.

"He looks fine," the vet said, turning to speak to her. "You can compete."

Gillian watched from the manger. "That's good. Thanks."

"You're welcome." He waved as he left.

Elizabeth peered over the edge of the manger at Gillian.

"Hawkeye may be fine. You, on the other hand, look awful."

12

The Big Show

Your class starts in two hours. You need to eat, dress and tack-up Hawkeye," Elizabeth said.

Gillian blinked up at her, then scrambled over the manger and dropped down beside her horse. "Is he really okay?"

Hawkeye nudged her and snorted impatiently.

"He's hungry," Carley said. "Always a good sign."

Gillian fetched a flake of hay for him and watched him eat it. She added electrolytes to a pail of water and offered it. Hawkeye drank thirstily, then raised his head for a moment and stared at Gillian.

"You look good." Gillian patted his neck. He ignored her and dipped his nose back into the bucket.

"Come on," Elizabeth said. "Breakfast for you."

After a quick trip to the motel to shower and change into her riding habit and a fast stop at the restaurant, Gillian returned to the barn to prepare Hawkeye.

"Return him to the outside corral after your class," the stable manager requested as she paused for a moment at the door of the stall in her endless pursuit of details.

"Fine," Gillian said from her position at Hawkeye's feet. "Thanks for the use of the stall."

"Please pay for it when you leave."

"Sure. Sure, I will," Gillian agreed.

Elizabeth, Gillian thought, I'm going to have to ask Elizabeth for the money. Her dad would pay Elizabeth back, Gillian knew, but everything about horses cost so much. Gillian snapped the stirrup down into position. Hawkeye's expenses weren't her responsibility. She needed to remember that. Right now, getting Hawkeye ready and doing well in the show were. She just wished she wasn't so tired!

The door of the stall creaked. Gillian looked up from the girth she was buckling to see Mike Yardy.

"Hi," she said unenthusiastically.

Mike was dressed today in a blue-black jacket, khaki jodhpurs, black hat and black boots. He was carrying his new Nikon camera complete with flash attachment and zoom lens; sophisticated, modern. It was probably his only friend. He looked like an international competitor, confident and … clean. Gillian glanced down at the spot of dirt on her tan jodhpurs. She brushed at it. Surely the judge wouldn't be able to see it.

"So your horse is better?" Mike asked.

Gillian nodded and slipped the bridle over Hawkeye's head.

"He'll probably be a little sluggish on the jumps. Some horses don't travel well. Maybe you should have come a day earlier." Mike studied Hawkeye.

More criticism. Slowly Gillian turned to face Mike. She was tired. She had to think about her class and the jumping pattern. Mike was no help. He never said anything positive or encouraging to her. He *always* criticized.

"I'm really busy right now, Mike," she said. "I'll see you later."

"You have a class right now, don't you?" he asked.

"That's right." Gillian picked up Hawkeye's reins and started forward. Mike stepped back.

"I can tell you how to set up for the jumps in this class," Mike offered as he walked beside her.

"No, thanks." Disappear, she said to herself, just disappear from my life.

"Why not? I'm good at this. You should listen to me," Mike persisted.

"I don't want to hear any criticism right now." She was going to stay calm. Mike was not going to upset her or make her nervous about this class. She wished he would go away or that she was a giant with an enormous paintbrush full of black paint and could reach into this barn and paint Mike right out of the scene.

He leaned closer. "You're too sensitive."

Gillian stopped, turned and looked directly into his eyes. "That's right, I am," she said quietly. "I'm sensitive. Hawkeye's sensitive. We don't need criticism. We don't want to hear it. Go away, Mike."

Mike flushed, backed up a step, then left her. Gillian led Hawkeye into the alley then out of the barn. She checked the girth to ensure that it was still tight, mounted and rode to the registration table.

She took her number from the registration clerk and, with one hand on the reins and one holding her number, rode over to Elizabeth's trailer.

Carley pinned the number on her back and Gillian did the same for Carley. When her class was called Gillian was ready — nervous, but ready.

The arena was much bigger than the ones at home. It had been freshly painted bright white. Huge red rosettes decorated the walls. Blue banners hung from the rafters. The crowd filled the stands on both sides of the ring. Everything was big, impressive and intimidating. The jumps seemed higher than the ones at home, the course more difficult. Gillian concentrated on remembering both the main course and the additional jump-off course. She joined the waiting line of competitors. She was third.

People stood near the horses. Many walked past and around them and some just stood nearby and watched. Most horses ignored the people, but occasionally one would twitch and stomp its feet. People didn't move away. No horse kicked out. They were used to the mixture of animals and people. Gillian was getting used to horses as well. She no longer worried that every horse but Hawkeye would hurt her. She couldn't remember when she had stopped being afraid, but sometime between her first competition and today she had lost her fear. It seemed to be in her past and a problem of her younger life.

Gillian sat comfortably in the saddle and let her eyes roam over the fans sitting in the bleachers watching the performances. She searched for Elizabeth and Carley and found them two-thirds of the way up in the middle section.

She smiled to herself. They would watch and appreciate anything she and Hawkeye did today. If her mother couldn't be here, she was glad Elizabeth and Carley were. In a way she felt as if her mother *were* with her, at least her good wishes were and that made a difference. Gillian's eyes moved down toward the ring. She saw the distinctive blue-black jacket of Mike Yardy on the ringside row. Why would he want to watch this class? He would only criticize everything she did. He irritated her. In some ways understanding Mike was like a composition problem in a painting where individual parts didn't fit quite right, making the whole picture wrong. He didn't make sense. Was she missing something important about him? Could he want attention the way Carley suggested? No, he wasn't that complicated. He just thought she was a bad rider and needed help. She stared at Mike's back for a moment, enlarging it in her mind, making it rotund, adding wings and feet until Mike became a giant, bluebottle fly.

"Number thirty-three," the PA announced.

"Come on, Hawkeye. Let's go." Gillian urged Hawkeye forward. Quickly she reviewed the jumping course in her mind and imagined herself sailing over the first set of poles. Success, she breathed to herself, visualize success. She pulled Hawkeye to a stop in front of the judge, saluted respectfully, then signalled Hawkeye to canter.

"Come on, sweetie. We are going to do it."

She set Hawkeye straight at the far centre fence. He cleared it easily. They circled at a slow canter and soared over the two centre fences.

Heels down, Gillian. Grip with your calves. Keep your hands still. Hawkeye showed no effects from his illness and jumped with enthusiasm.

The last two jumps seemed high, but Gillian set Hawkeye at them with confidence. They cleared the first fence easily. Hawkeye took three strides. Gillian leaned forward, anticipating, her mind already seeing the perfect jump. Suddenly a bright flash exploded beside her. Hawkeye shied, startled by the sudden light, and faltered. He broke stride, stumbled and crashed into the poles. Gillian sailed through the air over his head. She had a moment of bewildered expectancy before she landed on her shoulder with a hard thump in the sawdust on the other side of the fence.

For a second Gillian lay stunned, wondering how that had happened. Then she blinked and scrambled to her feet. One of the heavy poles that had been the top rung lay nearby, dislodged by Hawkeye's weight. Hawkeye stood on the other side, wide eyed and fearful, with the reins hanging down. He was shaking and snorting.

"Are you all right?" The ring attendant was beside her, bending toward her with concern. He seemed to be peering at her intently. Gillian noticed his round glasses and magnified blue eyes.

"Yes," she said shakily. "I'm fine, but my horse ..."

Another attendant grabbed Hawkeye's reins and began petting him. Hawkeye was still snorting but he seemed calmer. She needed to go to him.

She'd have to get back up on the saddle. She'd have to finish the course ... if she could just get her feet to move. She took two deep breaths and willed her feet to cooperate with her brain. The dirt was ochre-brown with a little black in it. The boards on the side of the ring were bright white. Gillian, get a grip, she told herself. You can't stand here and wonder how you would paint this scene. You are *in* this scene and you have to act.

"Are you sure you're all right?" the attendant asked. "That was a hard fall."

"I'm all right," Gillian said, ignoring him and looking at her horse.

She took one hesitant step, then another and slowly approached Hawkeye. She took the reins from the attendant and patted Hawkeye's neck.

"Are you hurt?" this attendant asked.

"No," Gillian replied without looking at him. He stepped back.

Gillian spoke to Hawkeye. "Are you all right, sweetheart?" She ran her hands down his legs and over his back. There were no cuts. She pulled on the reins and urged him to walk a few paces. He walked without limping. She looked over at the two attendants who were studying Hawkeye. "He's okay, isn't he?"

"He looks fine," the man with the glasses said. "You may compete."

Gillian nodded and then turned back to Hawkeye. She put her hands around his neck and gave him a quick hug, taking a few more deep breaths to calm herself. Then she mounted and trotted toward the end of the arena. There was a burst of applause from the stands. Her escape from injury pleased the crowd.

Gillian signalled Hawkeye into a slow canter and guided him in a wide circle at the end of the arena. He responded and seemed to become calmer with the familiar movements of the canter. Concentrate, Gillian. Hands steady. Heels down. Grip with your calves. By the time she had finished the circle, the ring attendants had replaced the top pole of the fence.

"Let's take those last two again. Okay, Hawkeye?" Gillian refused to think of anything but a smooth jump. Visualize it, she told herself.

Hawkeye approached the first jump with his usual competency, taking off from his back feet at exactly the right moment. He cleared the fence easily.

Three strides took them into position for the last fence. Gillian leaned forward. Hawkeye jumped it in effortless style. Gillian felt as if they had floated over it. She trotted out of the ring to huge applause. They had finished the course.

"We can't knock down fences and win, Hawkeye, but you were great, and so was I. As Carley would say, awesome, fantastic." She brushed sawdust from her hair and straightened her jacket. She'd done it. She'd completed the course even after she'd been thrown. For her, it was a win. Happiness bubbled up inside her and erupted in a huge grin.

13

The Real Winner

Several competitors called their congratulations to her. "Nice recovery," one girl said as Gillian trotted past.

Gillian enjoyed the warm regard, but she was thinking about the accident. It must have been a camera flash close to the ring at just the wrong moment that startled Hawkeye so badly.

She flexed the muscles of her shoulders. She was going to have a bruise there. She'd have to check Hawkeye's shoulder as well. He might have hurt himself when he hit the fence.

She had the saddle off Hawkeye's back and was checking him when Mike Yardy walked into the corral.

"Is he all right?" Mike asked.

Gillian nodded. "I think so. Nothing obvious anyway."

"I'm sorry, Gillian," he said quietly.

Gillian turned to stare at him. "Sorry? You're sorry?"

"Yeah, for scaring Hawkeye." Mike looked down at his boots and then slowly brought his eyes back to Gillian's. "I took a picture just as Hawkeye went into the jump. My camera's new, and I didn't know the flash would override my manual settings. I just —"

"Wait a minute!" Gillian felt anger rise, acidic, bitter and overwhelming. "Your camera flashed in Hawkeye's face and he stumbled. Have I got that right?"

Mike nodded.

"*You* caused Hawkeye to crash into the jump and me to fall?" She thought of how often Mike had caused her problems: criticizing her riding, offering her pinpricks of disapproval, getting in her way, annoying her, but this — causing her to fall — was far worse. "You, Mike Yardy, are trouble. Stay away from me."

"I'm sorry. The judges have been giving me a bad time for causing a problem, but it was an accident. Really. I'm trying to say that I'm sorry," Mike said again.

"Sorry doesn't cut it. Just stay away from me. You don't like me. You don't approve of me. Now you're really causing me trouble. Hawkeye could have been hurt. I could have been hurt."

"I like you," Mike said quietly.

"An accident? I can't believe that you — what did you say?"

"I said I like you," Mike said more boldly this time.

"You've got to be kidding." Gillian was astounded.

"You're smart. You're pretty. You're going to be a good rider." He smiled at her and shrugged. "I like you all right."

"Oh no." Gillian turned back to Hawkeye and started brushing his coat. "You don't like me."

"I do."

"This is a crazy conversation." She brushed so energetically that Hawkeye moved sideways in protest.

"I was trying to get your picture," Mike said, "when you went over the jump, I mean. I didn't know the camera would flash. I should have studied the manual better. I just wanted your picture and I didn't think about the flash."

"So everything — me going backside down in the dirt, Hawkeye crashing into the jump, that was all so you could have my picture?" Gillian faced Mike.

Mike looked away for a moment and then glanced back at her. "Right."

"What for, Mike? So you can throw darts at it?"

Mike was silent. Gillian was confused. Mike said he liked her and he definitely had wanted her picture, yet he criticized her all the time. With sudden decision, Gillian lifted the lid of the tack box, put her brush inside, closed the lid and sat on it.

"You tell me, Mike, what is this all about? Why do you bug me all the time? Why did you take my picture?"

"I told you. I like you, and I want you to like me," Mike said as if what he was saying should be obvious.

"That's it?" she asked, looking for more reasons, but Mike said nothing more. "That's dumb."

"Yeah … well … maybe it is dumb," Mike said miserably and sat on the other end of the box.

Gillian tilted her head and looked at him. She suddenly understood. His constant harassment was his way of trying to make contact with her. "Mike," she said gently, "you sure are going about this in the wrong way."

He nodded. "I guess so."

"Girls don't like to be criticized. No one does. So when you criticize me, I don't want to be around you. Understand?" This time it was Gillian who spoke as if what she was saying was simple.

Mike explained. "I thought you'd want to know what you were doing wrong so you could be better. And then sometimes, I just didn't know what to say."

"I have an instructor to tell me what I'm doing wrong. My friends don't have to 'teach' me, okay? Here's a rule for you, Mike, a social rule. Don't criticize your friends," Gillian said flatly, "or they won't stay friends."

Mike looked at her, his blue eyes serious. "I'd like to maybe …"

Gillian waited.

"I'm not good at being friends, but I'd like to try," he finally said.

Gillian thought about having Mike for a friend. He didn't have friends at the stable. Maybe he didn't have friends anywhere. She wasn't sure she wanted to be his only friend.

"A few ground rules then," Gillian said. "First, no criticism no matter how much more you know. Second, no put-downs."

"That's the same thing," Mike objected.

"More or less. And third, be positive and supportive."

Mike studied the shine on his boots. "I'm not sure I know how to do that."

"You learned to ride, didn't you?" Gillian was not going to let Mike feel sorry for himself.

"Sure I did," he said.

"You can learn this too." Gillian nodded encouragingly. "Think of it as learning the rules of the social ring the same way you learned the rules of the equestrian ring."

Carley climbed the fence and dropped onto the sawdust in front of them. "So, meat-face," she said to Mike. "You didn't get Gillian killed in the ring. Are you here to finish the job?"

Mike ran his hand over his short hair and glanced sideways at Gillian, then faced Carley. "Hey, I apologized."

"Big deal." Carley's fists were on her hips and she looked ready to fight.

"Back off, Carley. He apologized. He didn't realize his flash was on. He made a mistake." Gillian tried to calm her friend.

"Stupid twit," Carley said. "Gillian could have been killed and it's a miracle that Hawkeye wasn't injured."

Gillian reached up and took Carley's hand. She pulled her down beside her on the box and hugged her. "I'm okay. Thanks. Hawkeye's okay. I've fallen before. I'll fall again. Thanks for caring, but I'm okay."

Carley shuddered and then relaxed. "No thanks to klutz-city here."

Mike was on his feet now, sidling toward the fence.

"Mike!" Gillian called.

Mike stopped.

"Come back here." Gillian turned to Carley. "Mike has a problem, Carley, and we are going to help him with it."

Carley glanced at Mike, distrust written clearly on her face, but she cocked her head, prepared to listen to Gillian.

"You see," Gillian leaned toward Carley. "Mike needs to learn how to make friends."

"Hah!" Carley interrupted. "He should have learned that in kindergarten."

"He missed learning it in kindergarten," Gillian persisted. "He has to learn this in the same way I had to learn how to ride. He doesn't have a clue how to act or what to say or do."

"Hey," Mike protested. "I'm not a complete dud."

"You are. Trust me," Gillian continued. "So I thought you and I might be able to teach him how to act in social situations, how to make friends, how to be supportive, how to praise people, appreciate them, care about them."

Carley's eyes lit up with interest. "No kidding? Do you think we could?"

Gillian eyed Mike speculatively. "Maybe. Want to try?"

"Both of you?" Mike said in horror.

"It might work," Carley said. "We could start with standard phrases and make him memorize them."

"Yeah," Gillian said. "Things like, 'That was great,' 'Good try,' 'Nice work.' Just simple phrases to start."

"And we could build up to more complicated compliments like, 'Hey, Carley, you sure know how to get the best out of Jupiter.' Stuff like that."

"Well, I don't know ..." Mike began.

"Good idea," Gillian said. "And then maybe we could get him to give a little of his time to others, like help with the stable work or set up for shows."

Gillian and Carley stared at Mike as if they could see his future.

"You'll have to accept a little criticism at first, Mike. I don't see how we can avoid that, but you'll soon grow past it." Gillian was now sure that together she and Carley could make a difference in Mike's life. "You'll be a new man, Mike. Trust us."

Mike smiled the first genuine, warm smile that Gillian had ever seen on him. "If I live though it, I'll be a new man, Gill. If I live through it."

"Come on, Mike," Carley said. "We both have a class now. We can start our new project after I beat you."

"In your dreams, Mackenzie," Mike said. "You still ride too far ahead of the horse ..."

"Oh, no you don't, Mike," Gillian called after him. "She rides like an angel. Remember that."

She watched Mike and Carley walk toward the arena. Life might be different at the stables now if Mike stopped criticizing her.

She picked up the brush and turned back to finish grooming Hawkeye. Everything was different now.

So many things happened around horses. Gillian brushed with long, slow strokes. Was it the horses? Was there magic in the horses? Or was it the people who worked around horses? Maybe her dad was right. Maybe caring about Hawkeye, caring about riding and caring about doing well made a difference in the way she saw life.

"I guess painting isn't the only way to live in the world. What do you think, Hawkeye?"

She rubbed Hawkeye's forehead and hugged him. His breath warmed her shoulder as he nudged her gently. "I'd better call Mom. She'll want to know how we did. We were good, even fantastic." She patted his neck and rubbed his nose. "Next time, we'll win."